STORIES

FROM THE

TENANTS

DOWNSTAIRS

SIDIK FOFANA

SCRIBNER

New York London Toronto Sydney New Delhi

Scribner

An Imprint of Simon & Schuster, Inc.

1230 Avenue of the Americas

New York, NY 10020

First Scribner hardcover edition August 2022

For information about special discounts for bulk purchases,
please contact Simon & Schuster Special Sales at 1-866-506-1949
or business@simonandschuster.com.

The Simon & Schuster Speakers Bureau can bring authors to
your live event. For more information or to book an event,
contact the Simon & Schuster Speakers Bureau at 1-866-248-3049
or visit our website at www.simonspeakers.com.

Interior design by Kyle Kabel

Manufactured in the United States of America

1   3   5   7   9   10   8   6   4   2

Library of Congress Cataloging-in-Publication Data has been applied for.

ISBN 978-1-9821-4581-1
ISBN 978-1-9821-4583-5 (ebook)

for my dear Lindsay

Contents

Intro

Brown brothers, sisters, moms, brown peers
Lived in a building with their neighbors downstairs
Tryna stay alive, and make all their stars align
Scant money in a wad, the rent on their mind
A nose above the tide tryna stay afloat
On the edge but I hope I won't fold
Instead be like a pillar bout to crumble, but stay concrete
While a man is on my shoulder, all I want is peace
My skin is getting scaly and my boss is tryna rail me
I have to go work daily, saying feet don't yet fail me
Friendships, relationships, and 99 attacks
On my character, bills—and I'm Black
You see my hurt grin, you see my makeup, you see the
    stub from my job
You see the rainbow pop up in my scars
Everybody got a story, everybody got a tale
Question is: Is it despair or prevail?

The Rent Manual

days left: 10 . . . money you got: $0 . . . money you need: $350
    The slip is gonna come in the mail like it do every month, with the Lysol and the Save the Children envelope lookin regular as hell. It's gonna have your name, Michelle A. Sutton, on it. And it's gonna say balance. And it's gonna say when the balance due: first of the month.

Read the slip to yourself.

Scream, Shit, then stub your toe on the kitchen table.

The man in 14C gonna hit the wall.

Hit the wall back.

Banneker Terrace on 129th and Fred Doug ain't pretty, but it's home. Until now, it's been the same since you moved here when you was pregnant with Fortune. One long gray-ass building, twenty-five floors, three hundred suttin apartments. Four elevators that got minds of they own. Laundry full of machines that don't wash clothes right. Bingo room that the old folks hog up and a trash chute that smell like rotten milk.

Little bit of everybody here. Young people with GEDs. Old people with arthritis. Folks with child-support payments, uncles in jail, aunties on crack, cousins in the Bloods, sisters hoein. That's what everybody wanna concentrate on. The shit that be happenin only 1 percent of the time. Like that boy that got molested and thrown off the roof. Niggas still talk about that like it happened five times a week. Don't nobody wanna talk about the cookouts with beer and wings and aluminum flyin off the grill and you be smellin it and thinkin, Can I get a plate? The summertime when the souped-up Honda Civics bumpin Lil Wayne be vroomin thru the back parkin lot leavin tire marks. The dudes who be shirtless on small bikes tryna get Najee or some other snotnose to run to the store. How you take a foldin chair outside and cornrow people's hair from sunup to sundown for twenty-five dollars a pop and make a killin. Don't nobody wanna discuss that. You didn't come up here for no shoot-ups. You came here to make a good life on your own. You were twenty-five and you couldn't be livin with your mother and sisters in the Abernathy Houses no more. Plus, Swan, Fortune's father, is here.

You gonna go over there and live by yourself? your ma asked.

That's what I said, Ma, didn't I?

Chase after a man that don't want nothin to do with no baby? And how you gonna make for rent?

Imma get a job like responsible people.

I heard that before.

Remember them last words as you study that slip again. Don't try to hold the tears in, because you can't. Go in the bathroom. Rub the snot out your eye. Fortune gonna barge in as soon as you try to close the door.

How you thuin, Mommy?

Fine, baby.

You thon't look fine.

How you know? You a doctor?

I know suttin that make you happy.

What?

He gonna flap his wings goin, Earrr, earrr like Amelia Earhart. God bless that child. You didn't think nothin of it when he was three years old and lickin beads from the walls after his baths. A year later he was talkin funny and the doctor said he got lead poisonin. He asked, Did you expose him to lead? He said it like you was a trashy mother, and you blacked out. When you came to, there was three security guards with they hands on your titties, restrainin you.

Fortune still flappin around, flyin into your purse. Smack his hand. A ten-dollar bill you ain't know you had gonna drop out. It's a start. His backpack's open and there's a box that will spill out too.

What the hell is this?

Candies the school want us to sell.

What they need money for? I gave them money for uniforms last Tuesday.

I thon't know.

Can't stand that school. Always want money and it's always the special class they want it from.

Mommy, am I gonna sell it soon?

They don't want you to sell it, baby. They want me to.

Last month, instead a puttin money on the side, you bought this pair of gold-eagle bookends that you seen at Brookstone. Now did you need that? Do you even got books in the house? Or was it just suttin nobody got in they apartment, especially not Sheema? It ran you four hundred dollars and you said, That's it, after this I'm puttin part of my next check away.

You didn't. You bought Louis Vuitton bags, Jordans, leather booty pants. Open-toed spaghetti-strap shoes you ain't never wore and an Xbox you ain't never played. Social worker visited Fortune at home in apartment 14D, seen the fifty-inch TV on the wall next to Fortune's fingerprints and was like, That's a pretty pricey model. And you said, I worked real hard and I can buy whatever I want. Anything else?

days left: 8 . . . money you got: $10 . . . money you need: $340

Call Sheema up. She your bestie since ninth grade when y'all skipped eighth period together. Your English teacher called you two the Glamour Girls. When you did go to class, all you did was paint your nails and kiss up your lipstick. The assistant principal used to stare at your booties and the janitor got a hard-on one time and tried to follow y'all home. Sheema got a thick scar on her forehead cuz one of her drunk uncles burned her with a cigarette, but she still fine, almost finer than you.

Y'all are cool even though you graduated and she didn't. Even though you got a career waitressin and doin hair and she be in jail every full moon. You never been arrested. You been known to put your hands on dudes, but they don't never press charges. Everything you got is 100 percent you. You don't have problems. People supposed to tell you theirs. Mimi, my EBT card run out. Mimi, my baby girl swallowed roach poison. Mimi, come to my rent party.

Somehow Sheema got it together though. She got her daughter TiKai a Louis Vuitton rhinestone jacket and she got enough to pay you fifty a month to braid TiKai's hair.

How's it over at Banneker? she gonna ask on the phone all nosy. Heard they over there tryna nickel and dime people.

I ain't felt it to be honest.

A pause when y'all both is doin nothin but breathin on the line. Then Sheema gonna say, Saw your mom and sisters on they way to Costco. Your mother almost got hit by a car tryna wave me down. She heard about people bein pushed out and was like, How Mimi doin? I said, Fine, I guess. Then, she was like, No, really how she doin? Mimi, you did not tell me your mother had all them kids livin in that place.

Tell her your mother ain't crazy, she a witch who want you to become a welfare robot like her. She told you to drop outta school and you had to say no. She want you to be your sisters, makin macaroni and puttin they nasty undone toes on the food tray. If she and your sisters wanna sit around fat wit bad skin, watchin *SpongeBob* and waitin for some check, they can do that.

Meanwhile you gonna have saved up enough dough to move to Westchester. Hell, some of your sisters' kids might be able to move in, provided they stop with that mashin Cheerios all over the floor.

Sheema gonna ask, What time you want me and TiKai to come by?

Huh?

You still doin her hair, right?

Yeah.

Wednesday?

Make it Tuesday.

You love Sheema cuz she give you complete creative control over her daughter hair, but she don't know you bout to charge her a hundred dollars when you see her.

·　　·　　·

Roscoe's, where you work, is the banginest soul-food joint in all Harlem. Everybody done had theyselves a plate here. They got pictures all against the wall of Roscoe Sr. when he was alive. One wit Kareem Abdul-Jabbar. One wit that baldhead guy from the cop show. People see the wobbly tables and no AC and wanna grumble, but when that catfish come steamin out the back, it's a whole different story.

Greet your coworkers. What up, Mustafa. Hey, Laniece. Walk by Diabla and say nothin. That's your name for Vivian. The Dominicans taught you that.

Pretend to wipe down some tables and stack up some menus, but don't really work for the first few hours. A group of construction workers gonna come in at 11:30 wit hammers on they belts and paint in they fingernails. They got muscles and stomachs. One a them will be pickin his teeth like what he got between them is a piece of you.

Oh, this hard hat, he gonna say. This hat is to let pretty things like you know I got a job.

Laugh like it's the funniest shit you ever heard.

I like the ponytail and that tattoo up your leg, the other one gonna say.

Say thank you and tell him his biceps ain't bad, neither.

Bet they could lift you up and bounce you around.

Be like, Bet they could. Then act like your titties is loose and you can't control them.

I like this one, she fun. What's your name? Mimi? Mimi, we like you. You ain't afraid to talk.

Never forget the day four years ago on 110th and Fred Doug when Bernie, your boss-to-be, spotted you while you was in a hurry to scoop Fortune up from daycare. You was clickety-clackin up past the ninety-nine-cent bins by the Israelites with aluminum foil on they heads who always screamin out that God is Black. Bernie and his pasty self—this is before he got stank—flagged you down and was like, How would you like to be our franchise player? The next week, he put you on the three back tables and in one hour you had customers orderin Long Island Iced Teas and pork chops and applesauce, throwin up on theyselves. Customers wasn't requestin waitresses before you got there.

Anyway, serve those construction dudes they meal: smothered chicken, candy yams, and mac-and-cheese. With that extra cholesterol, Hard Hat will say. Watch them eat, cuss, and laugh like a pair a razors. When they done, lean in slow to scoop they plates and brush one a them on the back by accident on purpose.

Draw a heart on the bill and drop it on the table.

On his way out, Hard Hat will corner you by the buffet. Pretend you surprised.

We three put in twenty dollars each for your tip, he gonna say.

Look up and thank whoever there.

One catch, though.

What's that?

You gotta let me put it anywhere.

Say yeah before you can say no.

He might untie your apron and shove it down ya coochie. Wonder if you would slap him or not. Fortunately, he gonna tuck it in the part of ya apron where he think ya bra at and then pat it before he leave. Feel Diabla starin you down.

That's how much it cost to scoop sixty dollars in ten minutes.

But take it out ya apron and walk it over to the tip glass. Wait for your share at the end of the day, when Bernie count out all the money wit his pinkie. Call yourself a fool for obeyin this rule.

days left: 7 . . . money you got: $50 . . . money you need: $300

Go downstairs with Fortune to pay Swan a visit in 6B. His hallway is hot and it smell like brown lettuce. It's twelve o'clock but that muhfucka's in there. He prolly on worldstarhiphop.com, watchin the video of that dude shootin hisself on the elevator.

Don't knock on his door all haywire. Knock on it slow and sexy.

Chain latch, dead bolt, bottom lock. Swan in white socks and slippers, squintin like the hallway is blindin him. Don't hide the ten pounds you got on him.

And if I came upstairs bussin up in your crib, I'd be wrong, he gonna say.

Say, Fortune said he wanna see his daddy, so I took him to see his daddy.

Fortune never said that, and the way Swan scratchin the veins on his neck, he know that, too. You forgot how lean he is and how much muscle he got for those twiggy arms and how ugly but cute that scruff on his chin is. Let him pout wit those same black lips that used to kiss all up on your shoulder blade. Let him not say one word to you and pull his son in his apartment by the head. Then let him stand aside to allow you in, too, like he some gentleman.

People always wonder how he got you. He not a talker and parts of his face look swollen. But guess what? All the fine niggas ain't got self-esteem. It's always the niggas that got no business, the bums, the busted niggas, the jobless niggas, the all-the-above niggas that wanna spit. You was at Mayella's house party and all the brolic cats was huddled on the other side of the room on some middle-school shit and Swan was the only dude who brung you a beer.

He was like, Wanted to introduce myself. I swear that's all.

You thought it was mad cute when you shook his hand and it was all clammy.

You also thought it was cute the third time you was in his crib watchin *The Simpsons* and you pulled your panties down for him out the blue and his eyeballs was too wide to get it up. He called you up three times after that to apologize.

Last time he seent you, though, you had a tight pair of booty huggers wit your phone in the back pocket and he death-grilled you til you had to go in the bathroom and switch your phone to your front pocket.

When you and Fortune done settled in his mama livin room, he gonna whip you up a smudgy glass of Ovaltine and y'all gonna feel like a family again.

Be like, How you holdin up, Swan?

Fortune gonna say, Yeah, Swan, how you holdin up?

Hey, that's Daddy to you.

Sawwy.

He gonna turn to you and say, Maintainin.

Really? Seem like everybody runnin around this month like a chicken wit they head cut off.

Well, that's them.

Been three months since you been here, but his mama apartment ain't change much. She still holdin on to that old-ass vacuum by the futon and padlockin the food cabinet. A whole thing of paper towels is stacked up behind the front door. That got nothin to do with Swan. As far as everybody concerned, he a grown kid livin in his mama neat world.

Point at the new pair of Jordans wit fresh socks hangin out them in his hallway. Be like, Where you get them from?

They fell off the back of a truck.

Fell off the back of a truck, huh?

Don't start that.

Be like, I'm jus sayin I wish baby clothes fell off the back of a truck.

See, that's the bullshit—

Food and money for Fortune's doctor visits—

Mimi, I'm not doin this. I told you I been tryin. You want niggas to lie on applications? Fine, Imma write I wuhn't locked up. Imma put down I went to Harvard. Is that what you want?

I want you to try harder is what I want. Stop havin ya fifty-year-old mother work two jobs while you out thievin and sittin on ya ass, Swan. If I said, Swan, can you help Fortune sell the chocolates the school gave him, you would stand there lookin stupid.

Stop it.

No, Swan, you need to hear the truth about yourself every once in a while. You a piece a shit that can't contribute a hundred a month to support your son and his mother.

Stop it, Mimi.

You a coward, Swan. If your mama wasn't there workin at the school and the airport to put food in your sorry-ass mouth, you'd be—

Shut up! Shut the fuck up! You a hypocrite, Mimi. Let me ask you this. Why everybody in Banneker think you got it all together? Why I got niggas tellin me you goin around sayin, Fuck Swan, I don't need that nigga? Why I hear you goin around givin people advice on how to make rent?

He not gonna slap you or grab you up—Swan ain't like that—but he will open up the door's top lock and say nothin til you leave. And Fortune will be still sittin on the futon, bobbin to whatever music he got playin in his head.

Wring his arm up and say, Fortune, baby, we gotta go. When he say, But I thidn't play Swan in Sock'em Boppers yet, put your hands on your hips and say, Fortune.

As you halfway out the door, Swan gonna hit you wit the real dagger.

Bet you I'm the only nigga in here know you ain't paid your rent in five months.

People out there call you ghetto trash. How you got money to deck yourself out for the club but none to pay your bills? They be on TV shakin they heads. I don't get it, they say. It's ignorant. Just last month you bought a pair of stilettos and a Louis Vuitton suitcase for ya next trip to New Jersey. You bought the J.Lo perfume, the Beyoncé perfume, and the Miley Cyrus perfume. You bought them Bluetooth speakers at Best Buy (they was on sale so you stocked up wit five). You bought anklets from the African bazaar, that lamp wit the water fountain in it, that glass walrus you seen at Times Square, the moonwalk you rented for Fortune's seven-and-a-half birthday right after Sheema had thrown TiKai's six-and-a-half.

Every time you coughed up the money you said, That's it, I'm savin up from here on out, until they came out wit the new Prada belt line. Of course you could stop spendin. Eat no-name cereal and move to that house in Westchester sooner than you think. But it ain't worth comin out the house raggedy, not feelin good about yourself. You been thru that growin up. Your mama was buyin OshKosh B'Gosh and fondlin Goodwill bins for blouses that ended up scratchin ya shoulders. People on TV don't understand that and never will. They need to stop frontin like all people want in life is food and a roof.

You got Sheema comin in tomorrow. You gotta dial up Dary and inform him you don't need his services for this appointment.

Dary is the gay dude that live in 12H. When you first started doin hair on the side, he begged you to teach him. He said, Mimi, I can do this. I got dolls I been practicin on. Let me sit under your feet and watch you. You ain't gonna know I'm there. I swear, boo. He said, Mimi, you know ain't nobody in Banneker gonna let a man touch they hair.

You let him wash clients' hair and later, while you texturized and braided, had him put on the barrettes at the end, things like that. You hit him off wit twenty for his time cuz he got nothin else as far as you know.

Even though y'all apartments is two floors apart, swear you can hear his phone ringin thru the walls.

When he answer be like, Dary, this Mimi. I got good news for you.

Oh yeah?

Sheema pushed her appointment up to this Tuesday. I was callin to let you know I could take care of her myself.

He gonna be like, Oh no it's all right. I ain't doin nothin on Tuesday.

Be like, No, take the day off.

Then hang up the phone.

Guess which set a long eyelashes and angry cheekbones gonna be all up in your peephole five minutes later.

You doin me dirty, Mimi, he gonna say.

Laugh it off. Be like, I never seen somebody so mad about a day off.

You did this to me the last two times. You actin like you don't want me around.

I do, Dary, but remember this ain't a full-time job. You shadowin me.

Then why you tellin me not to come at all?

Ask him what he tryna say.

I'm sayin to your face and not on the phone that if you don't want me to come Tuesday, don't ask me to come any day no more.

Let him cross his arms and scrunch them eyebrows and glossy lips of his in your hallway like a dirty photograph.

Be like, That's fine, Dary. Do what you have to do.

Sheema is all about mirrors. Hand mirrors, vanity mirrors. It's like she exposed until she get to the next one. She think she prettier than you. She might be. While TiKai in your seat, ready to get her hair did, listen to Sheema brag.

All you gotta do, Sheema gonna say, is put notebook paper in the deposit envelope. Tell the ATM you puttin in five hundred and they gonna let you take out two hundred real dollars right there. Remember when that teacher at Sojourner called me a dumbass back in the day? Bet you he wouldn't of thought of that.

Stroke her. Be like, Mm-hmm. Mm-hmm. Wow. But don't say it dull, say it like, That's wonderful. Make her feel like she somebody, somebody who can get charged one hundred dollars for her daughter hair. You know it's workin cuz she start up about her diaper business.

I'm tellin you, Mimi, you need to come over and be one of my employees. I got workers gettin me diapers real cheap from all over: Key Food, CTown, Associated. I be sellin them almost full price at my building. I know—lazy heifers can't walk down the street when they out. I be cakin off this! I know it ain't for you, Ms. No Fingerprints.

Hold TiKai by the head. Let Fortune kick around the hair on the floor while you bring her to the kitchen sink to wash her hair.

Where's Dary? Sheema gonna ask. Come to think about it, I ain't seen him last time neither.

Be like, He said he don't wanna work for me no more.

What'd you do to that man?

I don't wanna talk about it.

Mimi, that man was learnin. He was conditionin. He was per-min. Blow-dryin sometimes. I was like, You go, boy. I almost might let you touch my hair.

I have a feelin we ain't gonna be speakin for a while.

Who else gonna teach him to do hair?

I said I didn't wanna talk about it.

Usually you give TiKai eight zigzag rows and then you string the rainbow barrettes at the end and charge your fifty. But do crowns today. Braid all her kinky hair into microbraids, then braid all the microbraids into two big braids that tie around her head. It's gonna take a long time and your fingers is gonna burn like hell afterward. When Sheema notice you takin more than the normal hour, she gonna say, You givin her suttin fancy today?

Be like, Yeah.

Straighten TiKai's head when it loll back and forth cuz she wanna sleep. Hard to believe this eight-year-old girl with her teeth shinin like tiny pearls be in school cussin and talkin bout boys' things. Let Sheema stretch her arms in the air and take her own nap on your couch. When you finish TiKai's last braid, put the lighter flame to both ends of the crowns to close them up. Flex out the pepper in ya joints. Brush the Indian extensions you weaved in TiKai's hair off ya lap and off the Velcro on TiKai's sneakers. After you done all that, be like, That'll be one hundred dollars.

Let Sheema's ice-grill burn a hole in your face like the one time in eleventh grade y'all fought over this boy named Sherman and she confronted you early in the mornin at the 125th train stop. She yanked the book bag off your back and emptied it out on the platform, and combs and pencils came pourin out onto the tracks.

She gonna say, It's supposed to be fifty.

Be like, I gave her crowns today.

You didn't tell me you was givin her that.

I told you I was givin her suttin special, Sheema. You was there the whole time.

Lean over TiKai and be like, Didn't I say I was gonna make you America's Next Top Model? Hold her shoulder til she nod.

Let Sheema squint hard like she's just found out suttin new about you.

Oh, I get it. You think I'm Dary. I'm not Dary, Mimi.

She gonna laugh in your face. It will sting you.

Say, You payin me or not?

Oh, I am. I got it right here. Wit room left to spare. Mattafact, Imma pay you and my rent today. Early.

She gonna pull five twenties out her purse and stick it in an empty plastic cup by your foldin chair. Sheema gonna yank TiKai's hand and be like, Let's go.

days left: 4 . . . money you got: $150 . . . money you need: $200

They got a meetin at the 135th Street YMCA wit the buildin's tenant ladies. What's it gonna solve, not much, but you need to say you did suttin. Attend it, but don't tell nobody. It will be at 6:00, so you gotta hightail your ass to Fortune's after-school and drag his big-headed self there. Inside they got a loudspeaker up and some rows of metal chairs and a table of muffins and orange juice under a basketball hoop. It won't be like the rallies on TV. Ain't no signs and chants. Ain't no cameras.

The way those ratchet old ladies had flung the flyer at your face when you was in the Banneker lobby made it feel like you was the problem. They like a gang with they nasty purple toenails and they earrings shaped like Africa and they wrinkled skin smellin like black soap. Think just cuz they retired from twenty-five years of answerin telephones, it's now they turn to be the ones dialin.

The young girl Quanneisha was the only one who pretended you might wanna know what it was about.

And that's how you here. You, Fortune—he climbin from chair to chair before you can snatch him—a Muslim brother wit a kufi, and a girl wit a tape recorder and a notepad.

Before the meetin start, mess around wit your phone to kill time. Google houses in the suburbs. Go to Images. Stop at one in some place called Wappinger with the redbrick and big-ass windows in the front like a wide-open eye. It got pools and shrubs and seem like it come with its own white snow and two rooms for everybody. Probably could open your hair shop in the basement and won't have to leave home. Fuck around and give Sheema a discount and hire Dary full-time and kill him wit kindness. Might could even sit Swan's ass in the house like a kept man. Fortune and his friends from school could play hide-and-seek and be anywhere—not like you and your sisters, who could only be in the closet with the leftover Christmas stuff or under the bed if you push the baby stroller all the way to the back wall.

Interruptin all this is Emeraldine, the head lady with tube socks straight out a exercise video.

This is the year, she gonna say while the mic is in front of her squeakin. This is the year we gonna fight for you like we never fought before.

Boo!

That's the dude in a kufi from a few rows back.

No disrespect, sister, but when's the last time you all did anything for us?

Think in your head, Damn, this shit might be better than the movies, but don't clap. Watch Emeraldine shake her head like she starin at a bunch of sorry constituents.

Take a second to look out the window and see what's coming from a mile away. This building is under new ownership and they're drooling for Manhattan prices. The city can only protect us so much now. What you have is valuable is all we're saying and they won't look you in the eye when they take it. They'll tell you you don't have secession rights. Bump your rent a teeny bit. Evict you right on time when before they would have dragged it out. All within the confines of the law. We just gettin you ready to deal with the slithering in the grass.

The dude in the kufi again.

We spose to believe that?

Excuse me.

Cons can come from your own kin.

He gonna stand up and take off his kufi for a second and massage his head.

We give y'all money for raffles every year and not one of us here ever won it. Wouldn't be surprised if y'all with the yakubs waitin for us to get tossed out so y'all can say I told you so.

Everybody gonna get quiet cuz he went there. A couple people gonna nod they heads like he Malcolm X.

As long as we stay unified, you got nothing to worry about. But. I'd be wrong if I didn't warn you—

Feel the groans around you.

Make sure you caught up with your statements is all we're saying. Make sure all those ducks is straight. It used to be you could slide with being a few months behind, but now they might start paperwork right away, so they can bump you over and charge the next one market price.

Swallow hard when you hear that.

Everything gonna be normal right after that like nothing happened. She gonna go on about knitting classes and newborns we all gotta take time to bless. Some volunteer gonna come up and say that they put up a fresh wall of paint on the sixteenth floor like that's suttin that gotta be announced. Other than the custodian at the entrance spottin you in the second row and gettin lost in your titties, wasn't nothin to remember.

When the meetin adjourn, get the hell out of there.

Emeraldine is gonna block the exit. She won the citywide gardenin contest for high-rises and her name got printed in the *Amsterdam News*, so she gotta put it in everything she do.

What apartment you in?

None of your business.

She gonna hold your shoulder.

Be like, Get your hands off me.

I was tryna be polite. You Michelle A. Sutton, correct?

Don't say nothin.

Yeah, you is all right. Michelle A. Sutton in 14D, right? Mm-hmm. They got you listed here as five months in arrears. You on they list for eviction after this month. I can tell you that for a fact.

That's bull. I pay my rent every month.

That's what you tellin yourself?

I don't got time for old bitches playin games.

Hook Fortune around the waist, hold his backpack strap in your mouth, and march outta there. Hear Emeraldine's voice trailin after you.

You might wanna stop catchin attitudes and get your ass to more meetins. You might know your rights. What to do in case they ever wanted to start paperwork.

Don't leave your room for the rest of the day. Hold your heart every five minutes cuz it feels like too much blood is passin thru.

There'll be a plate of glazed biscuits and jambalaya leftover from work. Try to eat it, but you can't. Turn in bed. Get up. Peek down your bedroom window. Get tingly and numb when you think how hard your body might hit the ground. Know better than that and drag your ass back to bed. Nap and drool saliva on the pillow for two hours. Hold your chin and tell yourself you gotta at least drink some water.

In the fridge is the three boxes of candy Fortune gotta sell for the fundraiser.

Throw on suttin, anything, then wake your son up from his nap. Run up the stairs to the twenty-fifth floor, where the crack-heads jimmy the locks and be slidin beat-up mattresses into empty apartments. Knock on the door that got the most rustlin sounds comin out of it. Some light-skinned girl wit purple cuts on her arms and a bony nose gonna answer the door.

You can come on in, she gonna say, but Imma tell you right now Latrell's not sharin.

Be like, Oh no, I was wonderin if y'all wanted to buy chocolates.

Oh, shit-diggity. We love chocolates.

Let her touch Fortune on the cheek, it's only a touch, and fol-low her into a dark hallway. Two women with saggy titties and hair that could start a fire is on the kitchen floor playin hand-clappin games. They gonna point they finger at Fortune and he gonna go, Thon't point at me. People gonna crowd around you, and what they smell like is gonna make you sneeze. Show them the boxes. When they ask how much, be like, A dollar fifty.

Damn, they must be the good ones.

Take a second to be glad. Everybody know those chocolates go for a dollar. If it was any other floor, people'd give you that high nod, that nod that be like, Yeah, uh-huh, sure. But the crackheads, they oblivious. There's a whole livin room of them hunched over smoke and lighters. Let them buy two boxes off you like that. Watch them take crumpled bills out the bottom of they shoe. Make forty-five dollars. Who knew they had all that money? Chocolate is a meal for them.

Cake up. Lean against the wall and think, This is actually not a bad get-together.

One of the women with the saggy titties comin out they blouse gonna tap you on the shoulder. She gonna point to Fortune.

What he got? She mean how he talk.

Be like, Lead poisonin. And the school say he got ADHD.

How they know he ain't just a hyper child?

Teacher said he jumped on the table and said he was Batman. Said when he in the bathroom, he pull his pants all the way down to pee.

That don't mean nothin. Kids is different.

Be like, That's what I'm tryna say, and actually mean it.

days left: 3 . . . money you got: $195 . . . money you need: $155

Bernie will have all y'all, all the waiters and waitresses, the busboys and the cooks, lined up against the buffet glass—durin business hours, mind you. Last time he had people up against the glass he had said, By the end of this meetin three of y'all won't be employed here anymore, and the next day Melville was fired.

Bernie's forehead scrunched up, hair redder than usual. He feel like cuz he white and he tall and he got a certificate from night school, he can line people all up like that. Here's my niggas

I'm in charge of. Oh, but don't call him no racist—he voted for Kwame Wilkes.

Any other day, as soon as he off yappin, you goin la-la-la in your head, but today's different. You been late three out of the last five days and Laniece was this close to gettin caught movin your time card for you today.

Try your hardest to hear him over the industrial fan.

It's imperative that we function as a community, Bernie gonna say.

Think, Say it in plain English.

I consider my rules to be quite simple. You smile. You put the customers on a pedestal. You come to work on time. That's all. I don't like writing people up. I don't want to fire anybody. But sometimes I've found the only thing that works is making examples out of people. So Mimi. Step forward, please.

Every bone in your body will scream, Flee! Flee! But step up anyway. See Diabla grinnin and shakin her head. She the one who probably snitched about you, when she was pretendin to bring dirty plates to the kitchen just to see what time you came in. Hold her up by the throat in your head. Empty out your locker in your head, too.

Bernie go, Mimi, you didn't know I was watchin, did you?

He gonna put a finger on his glasses to push them on right.

A week ago, I saw Mimi take a sixty-dollar tip from three men on a work lunch. You know what she did? She put it in the tip cup like she was supposed to.

Catch Diabla's grin turn into a frown. Be surprised, then remember the construction workers Bernie talkin bout. Recall how that cash felt on your right titty, what you was willin to do for it. You don't deserve this praise. Wiggle your shoulders out from those rubber hands of his, but he gonna be like, It's okay.

People. I thought this was simple. Every single one of you agreed to this before your first day. Mimi deserved that money. Those men gave it to her. But she said, Hey, let me share this in case Vivian is having a slow night. A few of you haven't been doing that. You're taking Mimi's money and your own, and I'm sick of it.

He gonna slap one of the wobbly tables for emphasis. Watch it swing back and forth. Diabla gonna speak up.

But what if the customer tell you that tip's for you, don't share it?

Vivian, I don't care if they say that tip is for God, you put it in the tip cup.

Bernie gonna look at all of y'all.

This time, I know who the culprits are and I'm telling you, you have until the close of business today to put that money back. If not, you can hand in your apron right now.

Some customers will peep at y'all on the way to the bathroom, eyebrows wonderin. Your coworkers gonna mutter, roll they eyes. After the talk, everybody gonna go back to they Windex and windows, they spatulas and cleavers, they trays of sticky plates. Mustafa, the pudgy janitor who never hurt nobody, gonna grin at you mischievous and be like, They don't never catch Mimi slippin.

Let that warm you up—they still believe that about you.

At your apartment, run to the trash chute down the hallway with a tied-up bag, and come across somebody's furniture by the elevator. Four dinin chairs sittin on top of each other, wrapped in plastic.

A bird cage, an old White Pages, a tall, skinny, crooked lamp tied up in a cord, and a big-ass plant pot with the dirt still in it. It all belong to Miss Violetta in 14F, that woman who used to work a booth for the MTA.

She been in that apartment since before you got there. When the super called the cops on you for movin in after hours, she was the one who told your movin people, Stay where you is, and the cops said, Ma'am, we're givin the orders, and she sucked her teeth and told the movers ignore these fools and wheel in that girl's dresser, and the cops couldn't do nothin bout it. Them times you got carried away with one too many brews crosstown at Sheema's, she let Fortune sit in her livin room. You wasn't happy that she had him readin them Jehovah Witness cartoon books, but she the only one in this buildin who never called ya kid special.

She broke her back five years ago when she slipped on some antifreeze by the dumpster. It never healed right and she spent the last some-odd years hoppin around on one crutch and a few months ago a walker. She gonna push that into the hallway now, with a box a picture frames under her arm.

Say all casual to her, So you movin, movin?

I like adventures.

She gonna try to show you nothin but good nature, but concentrate on the shinin of her forehead and see the truth.

I'm not just sayin that. I really do love adventures. Shoot, I might end up in Florida.

Let it go.

Back in your apartment, stare at the ringin phone. Who the—? Pick it up. It's Emeraldine from the Committee of Concern.

This Michelle, right?

Her voice will sound grainy. She remind you of your grand-mother on your father's side, the one who tried to pull your permed hair out the tracks cuz it was unholy.

Wonder how she got your number. Was she listenin just now? Huff.

Ask her what she want.

I'm callin to ask if you gonna make rent this month.

First of all, that's none of your business.

Well, I know you seen people around here with boxes outside their door, right?

Nope.

We gotta act before it's droves of us. You understand, girl?

Nope.

Can you at least come to the next meetin so we can organize and fight this thang the right—

Nope.

Fine, Michelle. Go ahead and be brick-headed.

Yup.

At least let me give you the speech I gave everyone else on that list.

She sound like she rather you not pay rent so she could be right.

Make sure your belongings is bubble-wrapped when the con-stables come to check on you.

Let what she say enter you like a ghost. Run your finger thru the calendar above the cordless. This so real, suttin better happen.

.   .   .

Don't call it a rent party. Call it a get-together. When people ask what the five-dollar charge is for, be like, That's to pay for liqs, you alcoholic.

Don't invite Dary. Nobody from the Abernathy Houses or with the last name Sutton. Not Sheema neither.

Your mama threw these all the time at Weldon. You remember them like the first sip of wine your uncle Charles gave you. You and your sisters huggin your knees in the back room while the bass from the speakers was knockin y'all sippy cups over. Actin like you gotta pee so you can see who's out there. Some fat man and ya mama rubbin theirs guts together pretendin they dancin. That same fat guy tryna scoop you up later in the night, like, Dance wit me, Michelle.

Don't get no DJ, a boom box is fine. If the CDs skip, the CDs skip. Put out the bottles of E&J and 99 Bananas you got left over from New Year's. Sweep the carpet with the hill under it. Leave a bucket of soap and water under the wall of Fortune's fingerprints, but never get to it.

At seven, dance by yourself in the livin room and pretend like it don't matter when people come. At 8:30 your buzzer gonna go off for the first time. Think, That better be Swan. The buzzer gonna ring three, four times. Different people, but nobody to man the door. Flip the lid on Fortune's cap and snatch that kazoo out his mouth. Be like, Here.

Give him his hat back turned upside down.

Stand outside and ask people for they money.

Mommy, what I'm thuin?

You shuttin the hell up and standin out there with this sign is what.

Watch the hat in his hands keep fallin to the floor and his spit and the gums they comin from. Look at that head, and them beady beads. Maybe a pill of that medicine the doctors said give him won't hurt.

People will trickle in. Hey, Laniece, glad you could make it. Hey, Mustafa. Hey, Mayella from the eighth floor. When people ask where Sheema at say, Oh, she couldn't make it tonight. Soon you got a crowd. Play "Do Me!" by BBD. Don't worry if nobody dancin yet, they will.

Ah! It's hot as hell in here. Just like a crunk party should be.

But hold up, who all that comin thru the door? Heads from down the hall, the twenty-somethin floor, bogartin. Folks who said, I wanna party tonight and followed the first boom-bap they heard. Go over to slam the door in they face, but don't. Instead count them in your head. Be like, five, ten, fifteen, twenty dollars. The gay twins, Qua and Quen, who don't even live here, come in. Shit, you forgot not to invite them.

Qua gonna say, This is the fifth rent party I been to this month.

Quen gonna be like, No, this the sixth.

When Dary comin up?

He couldn't make it.

You lie, Mimi. We was with him in his apartment just now. He in there with his Katrez CDs all depressed. He told us what you did. That was fucked-up. But you know what, we not gonna trip. You'll get whatever's comin to you. I'll tell you this, though. We workin on his brand right now, girl. Watch out for it cuz you gonna be jealous.

Fortune must got at least a hundred in the hat by now, so say excuse me and run out to the hallway. People scruffin Fortune's hair, pinchin his cheek. Pull the hat and count. Only twenty dollars! Go back inside and confront niggas. Most a them leanin on the armoire drinkin from Styrofoam cups with your liquor in it. Peep Mustafa in the corner gettin blasted. Snatch his cup before he take his next sip.

Where your five dollars at?

You had liqs on the table. I figured you was covered.

Watch him dance away from you. Watch them all dance away. Watch them bankhead, tootsie roll, grind, and dip. Rest your head on the wall by your picture of Obama. Fortune gonna be in front of you throwin his hat in the air and tryna catch it. It will hit the bulb and coins gonna scatter all over the place. Send Fortune to his room and lay him on top a the coats smellin like leather and perfume. Pick up the coins and the balled-up wet napkins that been tossed next to them. Sit up against the wall and rub your temples. The laughter and the cussin will carry on regardless.

Sometime between when you put your head down and when you pick it back up, Swan gonna barge in, breath smellin sharp, dancin off beat. He with two dudes in North Faces with they hands in they side pockets.

Before he add to the body heat, pull him to the side and be like, Where the hell you been?

A little bit a this, a little bit a that.

Who these niggas with you?

Ernie and Bert. I don't know. They followed me in here.

Feel Fortune run from the bedroom and knock you over to hop on his father's back. Swan gonna pick him up and knock over bottles of 99 Bananas. Make a face while both of them laugh. Squeeze past all them hot bodies to your own damn kitchen to get a rag under your sink. Dab up that liquor off the carpet and—shit—somebody threw up in the corner by your flowerpot.

That's how the whole night gonna go. You make forty for rent, but somebody puts a dent in the foyer wall and your hundred-dollar TV-order blender seem to go missin. Blunts will light up in front a you and burn your eyes. Chips will spill on the floor and boots will crunch them up. Whack furniture, some freeloader who got no idea this is your crib will say. Before twelve, some heffa is gonna scream, Hit me, muhfucka!, and one of those dudes in a North Face with the side pockets is gonna be foamin at the mouth and the other is gonna be holdin him back sayin, Don't hit the bitch. The heffa gonna be like, Nigga, your breath stink and somebody gonna scream, Shit, he got a knife! Everybody will clear out then, leavin you wit Fortune, broken glass, and a slashed-up couch with fluff puffin out.

days left: 1 . . . money you got: $240 . . . money you need: $110

Some of the bills are soggy and torn at the edges, but they count. Stick the wad in the tape deck of that old Walkman you won't let go of. It was the only gift your eldest sister ever gave you—that and an Al B. Sure tape she dubbed off the radio. She said that was what good music was, but she better not catch you listenin to it at the same time as her. She had seen a mouse on her side of the bedroom—no surprise with all them Pop-Tart crumbs she left in her sheets—and took over your bed. Told you, Let me make it over for you, and like a fool you said, yeah. Then she started spillin nail polish on your bedspread and gossipin on the cordless about Rashawn. And when you rumbled back demandin your bed and knocked over her CD tower and cracked the jewel case to her Montell Jordan, she gripped you by the neck and you could feel the power of all that extra fat on her shoulders. She spit on you, and afterward you felt choked and spit on.

When you turned twenty, you had the movin van parked right by the back dumpster. The driver, some thirty-five-year-old who liked spittin loogies and chewin on mint sticks, was like, You called us all the way here for you to move up the street? And you said, Banneker is farther away than you think. That day you left, nobody got up for you in the livin room. Your mother and your four sisters, they heads was tilted around you tryna see *Wheel of Fortune*. But you played your part, gave them all stand-up two-arm hugs for the sittin-down one-arm hugs they gave you. But you also had vows. No matter what it was—paper plates, toilet paper, somebody birthday, somebody death day—you wasn't settin foot back in the Abernathy halls.

Your mother called you a couple times and it went straight to voice mail. Your voice mail said, Hair appointments is Thursday and the first three Saturdays in the month.

Now imagine if you picked up that phone and told her you gonna need to move back in indefinitely til you figure some things out. Imagine that first night when you open up the frigerator where they always let the drip hit the bottom shelf and it get on the fruit and everything get sticky. Imagine all that extra heat and Fortune seein your sisters walk around in they bras all day. The rust marks on the shower floor. Your sisters' kids trippin over video-game wires. The two TVs they got on at all times. Imagine eatin dinner at that apartment again, out of that greasy plastic Tupperware that still got spaghetti sauce on it even after you wash it. Imagine bein in the house with your mother's boyfriend and him tryna tell you when to go to bed.

On top of all that, your mama, who shake the lamp every time her feet touch the ground, will call your aunty.

Talkin bout, Tried to warn her it's tough out there. Had to open my arms wide like, Come here, baby.

It's lookin more and more like you actually gonna need Sheema.

Your Roscoe's check ain't due to you for a whole nother week and besides it's already spent. The diaper scheme is suttin you could do in a day and cake up and don't nobody got to know. Sheema would be bussin out her seams if you said sign me up. Bitch would stand there bein glad.

Dial her number and wait for her to pick up.

She gonna hear your voice and be like, I'm hangin up.

Be like, Sheema, I'm sorry you thought you was payin the regular price. I thought you seen the crowns I was givin her and you knew. Next time know that when I'm doin suttin special like that, that's what it is, boo-boo.

Hear nothin but her breath on the phone.

I'm hangin up, she gonna say again.

The way she say that, you can tell she on her couch in that slip with the pink toads on it, forcin TiKai to watch *Housewives*.

Be like, Dang, girl, give me a chance.

No, Mimi.

Oh yeah, bitch. We'll see about that.

Be like, Remember that time your uncle came home and we was like, Where the Now & Laters you was supposed to get us, and he was like, I'm sick a y'all always axin me for candy, and you was like, Where it at, where it at? and he was like, I'm tired of this. Then he started cryin! Remember that? Was like, Grown-ups need love too. Nigga said, Grown-ups need love too!

Hold the phone. Hold it til she start crackin up.

Be like, Sheema, you my best friend and all, but your uncle sound like a broken faucet. Like really, Sheema, he need to get that checked out. I'm concernt.

Reminisce about the good old ninth-grade days when y'all both liked this boy named Lavon who had braces.

You know I seen him in the *Post*? Muhfucka was goin around gropin people at Columbus Circle. Tell me why my phone rang, Would you accept a call from Lavon Carpenter from the Upstate Correctional Facility? And I was like, Hell na.

I woulda done the same thing.

Say, Don't be surprised, Sheema, if he get out and fiend for you more when he find out about all those businesses you got steamin.

Ha, I know, girl. That ATM shit—well, that shit is a onetime thing cuz they close your account after they give you the two hundred available-now dollars when they found out you ain't really deposit that thousand. But the diaper scheme—I got people eatin steak off that.

Act like you groanin.

Thank god for whoever invented diapers cuz them shits get used three times a day. I got customers payin twenty, thirty dollars for a pack. You could be cakin off this, too, Mimi.

Cut her off. Be like, Sign me up.

She gonna be like, What? Gonna ask if you playin like sixteen times. Answer each time with, You heard me.

The Chinese ladies be doin it all the time, she gonna say. Gettin diapers from the grocery store wit a whole bag a coupons they done clipped from magazines, newspapers, store circulars, all over. They up and down the aisle with glasses on, studyin them packages like serious textbooks, seein which brand match up and which don't. People shoutin, Watch where you goin, and the ladies be cussin right back at them in Chinese.

After they done got to the line and put all them diapers on the belt, the total be like one hundred suttin dollars. Then, wala, they whip out them coupons and the bill go all the way down to zero dollars—sometimes in the minuses! You should see them fluffin they bags. They got they chin up and they eyes is shootin lasers like, Fuck you, only this time they thinkin it in English.

Can you belee that? Sheema gonna say. You can get anything if your heart is cold enough.

She gonna explain the rest to you. Scoop up everything like you a baby chick gobblin up his mama's worms.

After goin back and forth with yourself, decide you gonna really do it. You ain't got a choice either how. How else you gonna hold on to a hundred ten dollars before the sun go down?

Take the crosstown bus with Fortune to the Fairway by the college. Don't go to the market up the street from Banneker cuz the nosy birds will see you and start chirpin. Go thru the slidin door and open your mouth at the museum of food in front of you. All the fruits on white ice, prices written in fancy chalk. The floors swept up and the air conditioner blowin. The stock boys wit they clean red aprons and combed hair. The ceilin speakers playin that girl who won all them Grammys.

Read the labels on everything. Coriander. Ghirardelli chocolate. Sparkling water. Fennel. Dill. Mint. California rolls. Garbanzo beans. Organic strawberries. All the shit that make white people live forever. Slap Fortune's hand when he try to put the ice in his mouth.

Ya mama brung you to a place like this when you was a kid. D'agostino's was the name of it. It was a few days after she got fired from the nursin home. She dragged ya ass down there, said, Mimi, today we gonna be right up there with the Joneses.

You was bumblin about in that store, watchin ya mama put pork chops in that cart and tangerine drink mix and pineapple Fanta and Sloppy Joe in a can and hot dogs that looked like fat thumbs and seein her cart was different from everybody elses. You remember the white girl cashier ringin it all up and ya mama givin her the EBT card and the white girl cashier bein like, I'm so sorry we don't take those and ya mama, who normally get a joy outta cussin folks to they face in front of other folks, startin to blush like the sun was only beamin on her forehead. You remember how kind all the employees was who was ready to put the food back and held the exit door open for y'all. Ya mama said nothin to you the whole bus ride, just kept hummin to herself.

After you do this diaper thing for Sheema and get your rent paid this month and stop wastin your money on frivolous things, you gonna be gettin your groceries in places like this all the time. It's gonna be when you and Swan and Fortune livin in Westchester under the same roof, or even before that, when y'all are the last ones standin at Banneker in a sea of whities. Swan gonna be stubborn at first, of course. He gonna turn to you under the chandelier and be like, What the fuck is this nasty soda water you servin and these lettuce dishes with no meat? But after you done made him a few plates, with the long french bread and olive oil, he won't be drinkin nothin but Perrier to go with it.

Take the ziplock bags with your coupons out one of ya duffel bags, the ones that you clipped last night from everywhere that had specials on Huggies. Get the ones that come like two hundred in a box, Sheema said. I only fuck with wholesale, you smell me? She the one who gave you the idea of bringin empty duffel bags so you can carry all them back, told you get like two-hundred, two-hundred-fifty-dollars' worth of diapers, and she gonna give you half right there. You was like, really, you gonna give me the money right there? I don't have to do shit? I don't have to wait til you sell them? She coughed up laughin, was like, You think I'm an amateur, huh?

While you triple-checkin' coupons, Fortune gonna knock over a can of asparagus. Pull him by his coat and say, Didn't I tell you to unbusy ya hands? Say it thru your teeth.

Mommy, I was flyin. I thidn't mean it.

Be like, I will knock you out in front of all these witnesses.

Bend down to that can on the floor. Pick it up, even though you afraid your skin might rub off on it. Watch Fortune run away like he got a cape on. Catch up to him and drag him to the diaper section. Let the nosy people around you be nosy.

Two guys with red aprons and price guns will smile at you.

Can we help you find something?

Be like, No, I don't need your help. Could you get out my face?

Thank you, or where your garbanzo beans at, is what you wanted to say, but you ain't used to this. You used to workers sweepin brooms right into you. Now these nice gentlemen is gonna look at you like you had a bad Christmas. They gonna think you Shavonne, Shalonda, Shaquanna. That hoodrat that'll bite they head off.

On the other side of the aisle, workers is sprinklin lettuce. A lady in a business blouse is holdin a red basket and squeezin lemons, a forty-somethin-year-old with an iPod on his sleeve and a whole joggin suit huggin his nuts, scoopin a thing a trail mix. There gonna be wood everywhere. Wood baskets of tomatoes, prices written on the wood. The whole place feel like one cold breezy-ass farm.

Get to the diaper section. Once you by yourself, stare at the mountain of diapers in front of you. You gonna need at least three different coupons for each item you pick out. A brand coupon, a newspaper coupon, and a triple coupon. Whatever it take for the cashier to ring two hundred dollars' worth of diapers for free.

Squint at the diapers. Squint harder at the print. Which ones was it: Newborn or toddler? Newborn or toddler? Toddler or newborn? Newborn? Toddler?

Decide it's newborn. Go through all the diapers row by row. Snug diapers, dry diapers, overnite diapers, ones that don't let pee out the side. Rub your forehead. Pull down a box with the cute white baby sittin on his ass. Wait, they all have white babies sittin on they ass. Pull it down anyway. Is that the one? The one you tried to copy back in the day when you tried to take a picture of Fortune smilin on his ass, but he kept reachin for the camera and messin you up like he doin now with these airplane noises. Stand still, Fortune! Pinch his ear hard and go, One more peep out of you.

The package on the top shelf will catch your eye. The Huggies box with 216 diapers in it. That one. They don't got ones in the box at CTown. The most they stock is the thirty pack, and that tiny thing be expensive as shit. Lay your purse on the floor, put the bag of coupons in Fortune's hands, stand on your tippytoes and jump, goddamn it!

Tap it until it fall down and catch it. It's the right one, hallelujah. Fish out four more. Get ready to tell Sheema you only did this to make her feel good about herself. Wonder how Swan and his mother are copin with maybe havin to move to a smaller spot downstairs. Sigh. Fish out one more pack. Turn around to leave the store.

No.

Feel all these paper shreds flying over you. Turn round and this is what you see: Fortune throwin paper in the air, jumpin thru them like clouds. Only when they flat on the floor do you realize that they your coupons—all torn up like pieces of your life.

Stuff the diapers in the duffels anyway.

You heard right. Do it.

Just know what's gonna go down next.

At the cash register, the white girl with the ponytail will say, How are you today?

You'll say, Fine, like that's your answer to every question so don't ask any more.

You'll notice the security guard at the exit. A brother like five years older than you who look like he might hold his job sacred. Also notice he can see all the way up the aisle you was at. The moment he lock eyes with you, he'll put his chin up and rub his throat. Feel like at any second you could fall into a puddle of yourself. He'll say, Ma'am—

In a small office downstairs with papers and cameras, he will ask you if you know shopliftin is a crime and you will look at him like, What kind of question is that? His phone will ring and instead of, Security, he will say, Loss Prevention. He'll move the diapers out of your hand. You won't be needin these, he'll say, and you'll say, I ain't afraid of jail. I'm afraid of bail.

Imagine this. Imagine Sheema later that night sayin, That's my bitch! Imagine envelopes from all the apartments bein slid under management's door this month. Imagine all this.

Then stuff another pack of diapers in Fortune's backpack.

Fortune gonna say, Mommy, what you thuin, what you thuin?

Be like, We spacemen, Fortune, and spacemen need supplies.

The Okiedoke

My nigga Boons came home on the fourth. I ain't seent the nigga in four years, so when I heard he was out I'm like, Imma scoop the nigga up first thing this evenin and welcome him back to the free world. A lot of shit done changed since he was locked up. We got ourselves a muhfuckin Black president for one.

I slide thru to his babymom's crib on East 116th. Buzzer broke so I gotta shout at the window and shit. Elevator broke so I gotta walk up creaky stairs, too. It don't matter. They doin it big up there. Mayella had the Welcome Home sign over the radiator. Wine coolers iced up in the trash can. I come in and see my nigga all tatted and brolic, veins up and down his neck. I'm like, Yo, that's my nigga. Made good use of the time.

He turn around and give me a look like, Is that my nigga Swan? Big daps. Big hugs.

Son, he say, you grew like two inches.

He six two and my ass is five eight on a good day. I'm like, Ha, you got jokes.

Truth to be told, streets was empty without Boons. Whole time I'm thinkin, Fuck all this song and tears bullshit, I can't wait to get my nigga out and reintroduce him to the world. The glitz and glam. Make sure he back in style. Let him know what it's like, now that we got a G in the White House.

Once everybody leave I finally get Boons alone. His babymom's in the livin room playin checkers with his daughter. I find Boons in they little back room, holdin up his old North Face at the sleeves, starin at it like it's one of God's great gifts and shit. When the moment right, I ask him about tonight's plans.

Yo my nigga, what we doin to celebrate? Anything you want. You wanna grab a steak? Midnight ball? Piff?

I close the door so Mayella don't hear. Pussy?

This nigga smile, put his hand on his chin like he thinkin. What this nigga say?

Chinese food.

The hell we gave those muhfuckas in the day. This one time we show up at Good Taste late night and just start bangin on that window in front of the counter. Guilt-trippin them like, Is this bullet-proof glass here? *Is this bulletproof glass?* Knockin shit off. Poor old Chinaman behind the window, waggin his finger sayin, No, no, not like that. His wife come out, wipe her hands on her apron all nervous and hug him. And we just hypin it up: Is you sayin we niggas that's gonna rob you? Huh? You understand English? *Speak.* And he lookin all helpless like all he want to do is sell General Tso's chicken and egg rolls to happy customers in the hood and make his five dollars a pop. Like the last thing he wanna do is offend niggas like us.

Me and Boons say, Mattafact, give me *all* your egg rolls. All your egg rolls is on the house tonight! And we ain't scared cuz even if someone dial the popo, they ain't comin to Harlem no time soon. But still the Chinaman do it. He call the five-O, and we *out.* Soon as we get to the park on Morningside, we start dyin. Boons say, You seent that nigga's face like that nigga seent a ghost. It looked like that nigga wanted to go back to Shanghai.

Now, though, I'm thinkin bout the Chinaman and his wife huggin him. What he must think about niggas now? He probably got a shotgun in the back like, I wish a nigga *would.*

Boons go, I was feenin for them Good Taste wings when I was in the bing. I'm tellin you, son, we need to hit them fools up.

He tryna make a scene over there, I know.

So I'm like, Let's swing by my crib, call Miller and them, tell him you home and shit, then bust your ass in *Call of Duty.*

Me and Boons walk down two-fifth to my crib. Whole time Boons is bumpin into incense and soap stands and stoppin Yellow Cabs when they had the green light. He yellin, Y'all done fucked up and let me back, New York! Y'all shoulda flushed me down the toilet when y'all had the chance! That's Boons, though. He the type to not learn shit in the bing. Muhfucka take everything for granted. Had himself a full ride to play ball at Syracuse, and now what?

I say, I know you seen it when the nigga got elected. Y'all musta been goin crazy like some Alcatraz shit when that happen.

Boons step in front of a cab at an intersection, raise his arms when the driver shine his brights and be like, Well, *go!*

But I been followin the nigga politics and Obama on some—

Damn nigga, Boons say. You act like niggas hit the law library or suttin up there. You already know how a nigga like me did my bid.

He lift his bicep so I see his arm chiseled and that dinky tattoo he used ta have done stretched.

So woomp, we get to my crib and shit. I live with momdukes over on 129th and Fred Doug in a three-bedroom at Banneker Terrace. Momdukes cheesin when she seen Boons. That's like her second son. She even used to go down to the Rucker to watch this nigga's games every now and then. She got Judge Joe Brown reruns on, and she hear Boons and come runnin out in her curls and give him one of them seesaw hugs, then step back to hold him at arm's length and have a look.

My boy, she say. Let me cook you suttin.

Na, Ms. Dallas, you ain't got to.

She smile at Boons like he her baby and finish buttonin up her uniform. She gotta work the graveyard over at the airport. I hate it cuz she don't put on no makeup and she be tyin her hair in them ugly buns. Plus they don't never give her a uniform that fit.

To me she say, Aight. Long as he don't mess up the couch, he can make himself at home.

Soon as she leave I hit the TV a few times so it don't be all squiggly. I flip the channels tryna get to the sports or suttin but stop at the C-SPAN to see our president. Back in the day, I'd be like skip, skip, but I be keepin it there a few seconds just to watch our nigga in a suit. I *love* that shit. He sayin suttin about Afghanistan. Sittin at a giant round table, everyone all dressed up, with they glasses of water, listenin to him. I guess I put it on too long cuz Boons go, How them whack-ass Knicks doin?

I shrug my shoulders about to tell him the bad news when *ding*, the buzzer rings. I say hello on the scratchy intercom and then I hear, Open up, bitch-ass nigga! Then a laugh. It's Miller, nigga, your muhfuckin worse nightmare.

When Miller come thru, he always clap the wall above my apartment door and leave smudges. He bony but mad tall, like six seven, so he think he can son you. Always palmin people on the head. Especially Boons.

Soon as Miller get a look at him, he say, You finally put on some muscle.

Boons shrug like, Whatever.

You work on that weak-ass jay of yours?

Haha, Boons say. You's a funny nigga.

There truth in that though. Boons, all-city as he was, recruited with a full ride and woomp de woom, never could beat Miller in a one-on-one. Miller never seen a real basketball jersey in his life. But what he do when he play Boons? Back him to the basket, trash-talk til Boons forget he the all-American and Miller the scrub from around-the-way. Which is how Miller got his name. From that Oreo-ass nigga from the Indiana Pacers who used to kill the Knicks during playoffs.

Boons still hush-mouthed so Miller decide to change the subject.

What you feenin for your first day out in the world?

I'm about to jump in before Boons gladly speak up: Chinese.

Déjà vu hit me. Coulda sworn we was in this apartment, same positions, Miller sittin on the couch about to grab the game con-troller. Wifebeaters and do-rags on, wastin our life. I mean don't get me wrong, I could drink til I earl and get head from stank bitches on the stairwell all night, but we been doin that for ten years and it make you think: Is that all the next ten years got in store for us? Is we just gonna be some herbs, smokin roaches and rubbin our hands whenever the heat bill ain't been paid? We use to clown the niggas in the orange hats at Mickey D's or in the shorts workin for UPS, call them Yessir Niggas. But I'd rock that all day now, but can't tell these niggas.

Miller and Boons lookin at a crinkled menu momdukes keep in the drawer. Slicin they hands together. Them teriyaki wings look good, son. With the soy sauce on the top, too, my nigga. Some pork fried rice. Word to, Miller say, and that duck sauce with it. You know what I mean, dunny? They cheesin hard, all happy and shit, get up and dap each other. Boons go, Make sure you tell them niggas give you a whole bag of that duck sauce. They be stingy with it. Miller take out his phone and holla at me, What you gettin?

Imma fuck with the wings and the fried rice, too, I say, all low.

Boons be like, And throw some egg rolls and chicken wings with that and some grape sodas.

And I go, Ease up, my G, we ain't gonna be able to pay for all that.

Boons look at Miller, and Miller and him look at me, and then Boons say mad serious, Who said niggas was paying for this?

The plan was this: cut some notebook paper to look like bills, sandwich that between a few dollars. Give the Chinaman a fake address so five-O don't come straight to your crib. Don't matter what you tell them. You could be like, Top floor, Empire State Buildin, and they'd go, Fifteen minutes. And when they give you the bags and say, Thirty dollars, you take the shit, give them the Monopoly money, be like, Okiedoke, and *skate*.

I tell Miller, Whatever, but in my head I'm like, This some real nigga shit here.

Miller go, Boons, I know your bitch ass is down.

Boons go, I'm with it.

We call the dude who own Good Taste Mr. Basinboy cuz whenever he pick up he always like, Whatyaaddress? And we go, Banneker Terrace apartment #6B. And he be like, B as in boy? And then we start dyin like, Yeah, b-as-in-boy, *basinboy*. Mad niggas used to straight up rob them back in the day on some bully shit, in my buildin and the one down the street. Call, order they food, Chinaman show up and they just snatch them bags and slam the door in his face. Then when he knock and shout and curse, they open they door back up with a knife or a burner like, Oh, can I help you? Chinaman shake his head and be out mad quick.

After a while them niggas wised up, started showin up to the door with two of they friends or better yet popo. But they never *not* show up. They never think, Aww, we dealin with reckless niggas. They always assume niggas is payin, and we'd be quick to call them busters racist if they didn't. Niggas open the door spectin a free meal and blam, they got a officer ready to put steel on they shit.

But me, I been payin for my meal for a while now cuz Mr. Basinboy is what my nigga in the Oval Office call workin-class folk. Nigga made me think about how Chinaman will answer the phones, take they order, and send the delivery boy, and that make me think the nigga ain't half bad, even if he be actin like Black folks be raisin his cholesterol level.

That shit boggle my mind. I seen the same delivery boy get robbed three different times, They know niggas is lurkin and they *still* be over here. And people wanna be at the bodega like, Arab this, Chinaman that.

But yeah, whatever. So Miller dial the number. Mr. Basinboy pick up.

Hello, he say, Good Taste.

And Miller go, I need a delivery.

Address?

129th and Convent. Then Miller wink at us cuz that's at the top of the hill. We gotta go around the park to get there.

Phone number?

Miller give him his cell.

Order?

Yeah lemme get a fried chicken wing plate. Lemme get a General Tso, like five grape sodas, one of them teriyaki joints. You gettin all this down?

Then Miller stop, press the phone to his chest, and turn to us. What the fuck y'all niggas want again?

Boons say his order, and by the way he say it you could see him in the cell wishin for this day.

Then I say mine.

Then Miller say it to Mr. Basinboy and go, Don't be stingy with the duck sauce. Last time y'all muhfuckas gypped us.

Mr. Basinboy go, Yes, yes, duck sauce, yes. Anything else?

And Miller go, Yeah, how much all that? Mr. Basinboy prolly tryna to press buttons and figure the shit out when Miller laugh and go, Never mind.

Eh? Chinaman say.

Never mind. We bout to pull the Okiedoke on you.

Okedo?

Just have our shit quick, Miller say.

Chinaman go, Twenty minutes.

Miller click his phone, start dyin. The Okedo!

Give niggas pounds all around.

I'm so quiet and deep in my self after that even Miller and Boons forget I'm in that room til Miller go, I know what will get niggas hungrier. Then he put two fingers to his mouth and suck air twice. A ounce of that good good, Miller say.

Ah yeah, Boons answer, and slap the couch loud. I'm down, too, but I ain't all about paradin the shit around. Boons usually got a stash in his sneaker box, but he ain't been in his room for three years now and he ain't got a dollar to his name. So I go to momdukes' room cuz she got a stash of her own under her mattress. I figure she won't get mad. Figure we got at least a month of her just bein happy Boons home.

Yeah, boy! Miller say when I come out with that green stack. He punch me in the shoulder. Don't act like you ain't ecstatic, nigga.

There we is. Hot as shit in the livin room. Boots on the furry rug. Gettin high under momdukes' pitcher of Jesus. Silent night out there on Fred Doug. So quiet you can hear a crackhead scream. Boons take a puff, look at it, pass it to me. I take a puff, look at it, pass it to Miller.

He take a puff, and when the weed settle into the air, into our lungs, he say to Boons, So you back, nigga. Look like you swole at least.

Miller pick up some pennies and throw them at Boons' chest.

See, Swan, Miller say, how them shits bounce off that nigga like *wham*.

Then to Boons he be like, You was prolly bussin them niggas in ball, too. Especially since a muhfucka like me wuhn't there.

Not even, Boons go. Heads in there gunnin for me since day one. But on some real shit tough, niggas wuhn't even thinkin about ball that first night. Niggas was screamin to the left of me, to the right. Bangin on they cells hard, son. Tryna get the first-time to fold and shit. I ain't even gonna front. I ain't step out of my shit the whole first day. Pissed on myself. Had that stank jumpsuit for the next three days. COs dyin on some, I can't believe this shit. Boons Marcel pissed himself. Syracuse Boons Marcel. I called the white nigga who recruited me the first night like, Get me outta here. He talkin bout, Da da da he gonna pray for me.

I close my eyes when Boons doin all this and block out his words. Block out everything but that piff in me. I don't wanna imagine my nigga like that. I wanna see that nigga hittin the law library. I did my time back in '03. Three to nine in Attica for armed robbery. Word to, my bid was like: college. I read that whole Malcolm X shit from front to back.

Miller grab the spliff out my hand, take two more puffs, put it down on the coffee table with the *Jet* magazines, his pick, and one of momdukes' church pamphlets. He get this smirk on his face and say to Boons, Bet you had to take a dick or two, huh?

Na, Boons say, all low, I wuhn't into all that. He put his head down. Miller look at me and wink.

The nerve of this nigga, I'm thinkin. I wanna grab the muhfucka by the neck and be like, Nigga, is you crazy? You ain't spose to ask niggas that. They just come home.

So I say, Miller.

And he say to me, What?

You blockin the TV.

He move, and Boons change the subject.

What you all been into?

Us? Miller say to him all jokey. We holdin it down. You know me. Still gettin head every day. Still smokin that good good obviously. Mama in my ear like, Go get you a job. Had me feelin guilty about that shit. Til I went to that chicken restaurant downtown, and they wanted niggas to wear a bird suit. I was like, Fuck that!

Boons start dyin like that the funniest thing he heard in a while, bringin his knees up to his stomach.

Mattafact, Miller continue, I robbed a nigga for an iPod and nine dollars later that day. A dude with a tie on and all that. I walked that nigga to the train, make sure ain't no cops involved and he talkin, Brother, lip all quiverin, we got a Black president now. I dead azz looked that muhfucka in the eye and was like, What the fuck that got to do with this?

Boons slappin the coffee table hard. The sticks and stems of the piff jumpin in the air. It ain't all that funny. But I guess it the weed or the way Boons is all shook up, so I let out a little suttin suttin, too.

Miller look at me. Don't you laugh neither, Swan.

Then he look at Boons, nod in my direction, say, This nigga be on that Black president shit, too. On that We-gotta-change-our-lives shit. But when it time to guzzle a forty down, Swan got his hand out too. When chicken heads come thru, he actin like he playin it cool, like he want no part of it, but then he be in line to get his dick sucked like the rest of us.

I go, It ain't like that.

It ain't?

I don't say shit. My high is gettin kilt.

When Dejenei came thru that time, did you or did you not let her dome you up?

I was just sayin, ventually niggas is gonna have to look at they-selves and—

Did you or did you not?

Boons is coughin up, shit so funny to him. I don't get it. Miller provin he a asshole that's all, bringin up shit that you shouldn't even bring up. So I just sit there lookin tight.

That's what I thought, Miller say. He go over to the couch

Boons is on and give him dap. Boons look at me with an expression like, I'm tryin not to laugh but this nigga *hilarious*.

And Swan was the fourth nigga, Miller say. She had all of us in her mouth before she went on your shit.

That's it for me. That make me feel some kind of way, so I stand up.

Where you goin? Miller say.

You talkin real greasy right now.

Miller stand up too. He so tall it hurt my neck to look him in the eye. But before he can say suttin back, Boons press a finger to his watch: the food.

Son, Miller say to me, we bout to pull this off.

Outside, on Fred Doug, an ambulance is goin *wayow-wayow*. The freaks is still out, no doubt, your crazies and bottle-huggers. Miller and Boons hustlin, me two steps behind.

We walk around the park, down 127th, then back up to 129th on the west side. We see the fence on the way up and Boons is like, Be ready to hop that shit. We'll cut thru the park on the way back.

You heard that? Miller say to me.

That nigga still don't get that I ain't got no words for him.

We pass some snotnoses on a stoop. Look like they playin Truth and Dare. One of the nappy-headed ones yell, Where y'all goin? Chinese food, Miller yell back and then keep movin. Then the leader go to his friends and say, They bout to pull the Okiedoke.

Then we see the delivery boy's bicycle. Parked on almost the white people's part of Harlem. He got one of them yellow adjustable caps and holdin two bags with smiley faces, just standin there like they wuhn't three niggas rollin up on him. Miller the first one to speak.

You got our food, right?

Chinaman go, Yes, yes, and hand them the two plastic bags.

And I think, Why they always handin the bags first when muhfuckas is gettin robbed left and right round here? I give the delivery boy a I'm-sorry look that's more like I know what's about to go down and I know how you gonna feel about it and he get the vibe I'm throwin but it's way too late cuz Miller done yanked the bags outta my man's hand and slapped the folded money in his palm and screamed, We out!

We out! We out! We out! I don't know why I'm runnin, but we all is, past the high-rises, the fire escapes, the graffiti, the r.i.p. murals. Past all the air conditioners in the cribs above, the snot-noses again, the nappy-headed one be like, They done did it, the muhfuckas pulled it off. I'm in last place, Miller and Boons dippin around the corner neck and neck. Can't tell who the all-American, who not. Delivery boy screamin suttin in Chinese, Miller screamin suttin at me, Boons screamin, Swan, hurry up, you slow muhfucka, loud enough to make a nigga start thinkin, How long I'm gonna be runnin like this? Every time I'm hungry?

The fence. At the top of St. Nick. It come up like a shadow. Miller must think he hear sirens cuz he scream, Popo! He take no chances. He hop the fence to the shortcut through the park, Boons followin, all sweaty. They on the other side now and Miller shout, Swan, get ya slow ass over here. But a nigga like me is tired.

Na, nigga.

Boons go, Quit playin around and hop that shit.

Imma walk around.

Miller chime in, You gonna what?

Here the keys. Imma walk around and meet y'all.

This nigga, Miller say. And then he and Boons dip off.

It's gonna be an extra three blocks—129th, 128th, 127th, and back around the park—til I get back to momdukes' place. But the breeze kick in, and I get to take in my hood. The night buses, the pit bulls barkin, the niggas in fitteds, the chicks in stilettos, and I think about how not too long ago niggas was in the streets when that nigga was elected. Cars honkin. I had me a beer, guzzlin that shit down, just soakin that shit in. Cop car roll up slow on me but they just stuck they head out the window and was like, He did it, he did it.

Fifteen minutes later, I meet Boons and Miller at the apartment. Of course they on the couch dyin. As soon as I slam the door, Miller go, Scuse me, prima donna, and Boons go to him like, That nigga Swan on his own schedule.

I take a seat.

Miller go, Bet you that nigga gonna grab a wing, though. Bet you.

The food all on the coffee table. They done ate half the wings. Sauce stickin on the foam. Grape soda been out a little while, water drippin on the can. It's thick as a muhfucka in the livin room. I can feel all the sweat they brung from outside. Miller's hoodie on the couch next to him. They both in they wifebeaters, wipin they beaded foreheads. But that's them. I don't mind the heat. Just had my ass a breezy walk.

And they right. I reach for one of them containers and grab me a chicken wing and take a can of soda. Click. Sip. Bite. Chew. Suttin's on the TV. Suttin's goin on outside. Suttin's goin on with the tenants downstairs, but none of that matters. Boons and Miller talkin bout how it's time to get some skins, but I'm only hearin bits and pieces. My jacket's still on. And for now I'm cool with the fact I ain't got to take it off yet.

Ms. Dallas

The first day of school they assigned me and my student Cassius with the new seventh-grade teacher, Mr. Broderick, for fifth period. All I had to do was look him up and down once to tell he was gonna be a mess. White boy with no hair on his chin, smilin at his books.

He didn't have no icebreakers, no *Imma get to know you*. Only suttin written on the board: Steinbeck and Society. No *Lesson AIM*, no *Do Now* or nothin. So I push Cassius in his seat and go up to him.

Excuse me, Mister—?

Broderick.

Excuse, Mr. Brother Rick, what's the lesson for—

And you?

Sorry—Ms. Dallas. I was wonderin what your lesson was so I can get little Cassius situated.

It's on the board.

Oh. What do they have to do?

Nothing. It's a talk.

Oh.

It'll be fun.

The bell rang and he chopped up his papers. The kids come kinda quiet, kinda loud. Braids, extensions, weaves, naps, lice, ringworms. Black, Nigerian, Jamaican, Dominican, Puerto Rican, Muslim, from the block, fresh off the boat.

Good morning, class, he say.

One kid go, Waddup! And the rest of them is like, Good morning, like they in front of an open casket.

Now that's a lukewarm greeting. Let's try that again. Good *morn*ing, class.

Then they all wanna climb up on each other and scream.

That's better, he say.

Then he dive right in, talkin suttin about Depression-era this and migrant that. He in a full corduroy suit, his sweat nearly heatin up the whole damn room. The kids is quiet, even Lashaun who they call Kowboy cuz of his sideburns, and Mr. Broderick crane his head and catch my eye to make sure I see that. He don't know his words is goin straight thru they foreheads and hittin nothin on the way out.

For homework, I'd like you to read the first thirty pages in *Of Mice and Men*. It's a quick read.

Me, I say nothin, knowin some of these kids couldn't get thru thirty pages of *The Cat in the Hat*.

The other day, sittin in the teachers lounge, I said, Eighth-grade Amir assaulted a mailman and that's why he wasn't in school for three weeks. They was like, Ms. Dallas, don't you mean sixth-grade Amir? and I was like, Whichever. When you been in the schools for fifteen years, that stuff happens.

My name is Verona Dallas and guess my age. Well, I'm not tellin. I will say I got a twenty-five-year-old son named Swan and a twenty-two-year-old daughter named Jubilation, a fancy word that mean happiness. Nights I work at the airport doin security, and during the day I work at Sojourner Truth Middle School across the street from the buildin I've lived at ever since I was nineteen.

I'm a paraprofessional. If you a para, they assign you a kid. Either the kid got thinkin issues or ADHD or fight too much, and they pay you peanuts compared to what it should be to sit with them all day to keep them from flunkin out or killin or shittin their draws. This year they put me with this boy named Cassius. Only reason he need a para is cuz his hands go like this, like tremors. But really I do a little bit of this, a little bit of that. Put the flowers up for the Pan-African Gala, or sometimes they got me in the office stuffin envelopes, or in the lunchroom mindin the whole thing.

The kids mostly call me Ms., or they confuse me with the other para, Ms. Exum, cuz they think anybody heavyset with orange lipstick don't care what you call them. Some of them say, Mornin. Ask me if I want some of they bacon-egg-and-cheese. The boys'll ask if I'm married or if I think they cute, and that's when I gotta shut it on down.

Last year the people over at the superintendent's office gave our school a D. Said too many kids is gettin fourteens on the state tests and put us on probation. Said if they come back in March to another circus, we could say sayonara to everything.

Mr. Broderick went to Harvard. You know that cuz he say the word five times a minute. Durin in-service two days before school started, when we was all introducin ourselves, Ms. Botelli stood up and said, Well, one thing you all should know about me is I need my coffee, and while everyone was fake-laughin, Mr. Broderick turnt around and said to her, At Harvard we lived on coffee.

Today, I see he finally add some spruce to his desk. In the right corner, by the computer, he put up pictures of him and his college friends with they arms wrapped around each other and with moptop hair like him. And where Ms. Chad used to hang her dry cleanin reminders, he tack up some quote that say, Learning never exhausts the mind.

Me and Cassius come in, then the rest of the kids. They quiet, but I got suttin on every last one of them. Darryl stutters when he cussin you out. Winnette can't leave nobody's mother alone. Najee and Kowboy like roastin each other durin somebody lesson. Kimberly always wanna finish her work early so she can tell you how dumb you are. Saiwan like holdin down the left side of his nose and blowin loud snot out the other. Kyia wanna ask for the bathroom pass every period and when she come back wanna fling the door open so it hit the wall. But it's the first week of school: I guess they still sniffin people out.

Mr. Broderick go, Let's discuss the beginning of Steinbeck's beautiful book, shall we? But everybody, myself included, was down at his sneakers, wonderin how he gonna wear a shirt and tie, then have sneakers that look like they been stompin in swamp tide.

Who wants to start? Observations.

I'm disappointed cuz this is the book about that slow man goin around killin everything and all Broderick wanna do is talk about it. Ms. Chad called out sick every other day, but at least she put the class in straw costumes like ranch workers, then in lawyer suits and had them arguin whether the one with sense shoulda gone to jail for shootin the slow one. Then, she had them pretendin the characters was on *Oprah*, talkin bout they problems, which was fun til Daquan asked the girl who was playin the wife if the slow one had a big dick.

None of them raise they hands cuz ain't none of them read. This is where Mr. Broderick spose to refer to me and say, Ms. Dallas, you been here, why these kids didn't read, and I'm spose to go, Cuz a lot of them can't.

Ms. Dallas? he say, holdin out two sheets of paper with an article on them.

Yes, I say.

Can you make me thirty copies of this, please?

Swan say, Ma, you need to let him know that's not your job.

Yeah, Ma, Juju say, he your coworker, not your boss.

They gung ho cuz I took the padlock off the cabinet and let them put the last of the vanilla wafers in the ice cream. I run a tight ship. We use plastic cups. Yep, you go in the drawer, fix a piece of maskin tape on it, write your name on it, and everybody know that's your cup. My kids is fully grown, but they know they gotta vacuum and plug it up by the futon when they done. That's how I can keep this place halfway neat. I gotta work on the light bulb situation—two hundred watts in there and it's still too dark. Must be suttin with the wirin.

To Swan I say, I tried to tell him these kids is fidgety and he might wanna switch it up, but no, it's like he think he at some podium.

Swan go, Fuck him. I mean—sorry, Ma—forget him. Let them kids run his ass up the wall. It ain't your problem. Member how I used to do? Member when you used to have to come from down the hall to get me?

It *is* my problem, Swan.

Banneker Terrace—the buildin I been residin in for twenty-six years—is forcin me out my apartment and into a smaller one. The buildin figured now is the time they wanna start doin renovations on our dime, and my monthly contribution went up as far as the law say they can hike it. I been sincere with my rent every month, even when my kids' father mixed hisself up in this kung fu business and moved by hisself to the Bronx to train for Shanghai. Now I jus can't, and they don't wanna extend no type of branch. Did I complain when the brown stuff was comin back up the toilet? When I seen the dead pigeon wings in the laundry? Did they show gratitude for that? Apparently, my pedigree mean nothin.

Last year Ms. Chalmers, the principal, had me in the office cuz I fell asleep in one of the classes. Saliva came out my mouth and somebody yelled, Eww! and that started a whole bunch of dominos. Then she had me in the office again cuz I was painting my fingernails in the class and flippin thru a Victoria Secret. Then she called me in cuz I ordered Chinese food durin a test.

Ms. Chalmers, from behind a whole heap of papers and a beepin computer, asked, Where did you ever get the notion that this was okay?

She tried to act like it was me who was out of her own natural mind, like everybody wasn't already goin haywire durin that sorry-ass test, like I woulda dare done the same thing in Ms. Harrison class where everybody hushed up and afraid to breathe wrong. I told her as much.

When the superintendents came by last year with they clipboards and basically wrote down this place was a jungle, they closed Ms. Chalmers' office door and pressed her with an ultimatum. Said suttin better revolutionize fast, so she fired Ms. Chiku and Mr. Pierre, with his no-underwear-wearin, breath-smellin-like-Seagram's self. Issue was, who gonna teach in they place at a school with a rep like Sojourner's? Fresh-eyed white girls and boys like Mr. Broderick, who save our souls and treat children from Harlem like they children from Botswana, is who.

When I was in school, I was the one sellin Newports out my backpack. I was the one cussin out teachers. I remember we had this one Chinese lady teachin us algebra. I had foundt a picture of her and her husband dressed in Chinese clothes on they weddin day and I passed it around and everybody was laughin, and she started cryin. I knew how to test people then, and I know when these bug-eyed kids is testin people now.

After spendin two weeks askin the class questions about a book ain't none of them read, Mr. Broderick decide he wanna end the *Of Mice and Men* discussion with askin more questions. Everybody book is out on they desks. Half of them is closed and the pages look as fresh as when they was first stamped. Some students is listenin. Some is wipin they face down every two seconds. Some got they feet up on the desk furniture. Some is wearin they jacket sleeves, even though this sposed to be a uniform school.

Do you think George did the right thing by killing Lennie? Mr. Broderick asked.

Nobody raise they hand.

Do you know anyone in your life who has a mental illness that wasn't treated?

Kowboy raise his hand.

I know this retarded boy named Ay Dawan.

Everybody turn to Ay Dawan and bust out laughin.

Mr. Broderick go, First of all, Lashaun, that's unacceptable behavior. Second, we don't say *retarded*.

So what is he then?

Everybody go fallin out again.

We say *mentally challenged*. Which Ay Dawan *isn't*.

Kimberly raise her hand like, Ooh, ooh, pick me.

She go, George couldn't do nothin about it because they was both poor so they had to keep workin and workin and bein treated bad.

Everybody grunt at Ms. Show-Off, includin me.

Mr. Broderick ask, Were the men on the ranch right for going after Lennie?

Kimberly say, No, cuz he didn't know what he was doin.

The class meanwhile like, You buggin, he knownt enough to kill a girl. How you sound.

Kimberly say back, They knew he had problems, he was slow. They shoulda helped him a long time ago.

Mr. Broderick nodded and shook his pointy finger at that and Kimberly stuck her tongue out to the rest of the class.

The class: You think you white. You not white. You light-skinned.

Ay Dawan raise his hand. Can I use the restroom? See, that's how it start. First thing, they goin to go to the bathroom whenever they have the gall, next thing, they hangin off the chandelier if we had one. I know all the tricks.

I intervened like I should have.

Ay Dawan, now you know you don't need to go to no restroom. Sit your butt down.

Naturally, Ay Dawan turn to Mr. Broderick to save him.

Mr. Broderick shoot me this cold death stare and go, Ay Dawan, you may go.

They fresh out of college with a magic wand. They done read all the articles. Believed every news show that said public schools and teachers in the ghetto is fallin apart like pie crust. Watched every feel-good movie, thinkin at twenty-two they can come in here and set the world right in minutes. All the while, they bidin they time til law school. Mr. Broderick bout Swan's age hisself. They play hangman in the teacher lounge and crack on each other's mothers just like they students. Sooner or later, the realness of the world come crashin down on them, and then they'll sit there wonderin why they stuck in the middle of Harlem. But ain't nobody surprised, Mr. Broderick. Cuz people like you run off raggedy when they smell fire.

Next two months ain't no different, with *Robinson Crusoe*, so I mind my own business. Today I foiled up some leftover turkey legs and was sellin them in the school store for three dollars. Usually I do them with the bisque and the bacon bits on top, but this time I made them with honey and pepper and steamed collards next to them for a whole hour. I call it my pre-Thanksgiving. Mr. Nyim bought a plate and seconds. So did Ms. Harrison. They tried to write me up for that, too, but they can't get enough of it their damn selves. I carry a pro bono plate in the teacher lounge for

Mr. Broderick. Sure enough, he in there in front of his laptop, scratchin his beard and scratchin his foot with the other foot. They say he from Washington as in the Washington that's on the other side of the country.

Mr. Broderick, I go. Thought you'd appreciate this.

The turkey legs is right in front of him steamin, spices smellin good. Somehow he only wanna concentrate on the water drippin off the wrappin and I think, Maybe I shoulda put it in a fancier dish and tied it up with a bow.

No thanks, he say, and go right back to typin.

You sure? These is goin quick.

They *are* going quick, huh?

He an asshole.

We get our first big snow beginnin of December. I go to the teacher lounge to coordinate the white elephant cuz the white elephant is my thing. I like to put up this bulletin with brown paper bags and color them up like Santa's sacks. In it is slips of paper with the instructions of the price limit and when the due date for the gift is. All the young teachers is laughin in some kinda uproar. They in the back where they store the two computers and the paper cutter that take so long to cut on. I'm in the front part where sometimes people like to close the glass door and eat whatever they brought in peace.

They gigglin out of the chairs and I'm like, Oh, that's cute, until I actually hear what's bein talked about.

My para does Blossom's quizzes for her—and half the answers are still wrong!

My para puts her open-toed feet on the desks.

My para says, "no pun intended" when she means "no offense."

They laughter crashin all over the place. It was so loud you could barely hear the microwave and the Xerox runnin off copies.

And then Mr. Broderick.

Mine's a piece of work. They really ought to do a better job of screenin these people.

When I heard that, I almost stapled my finger to the daggone board, but I also nodded my head and said to myself, Oh that's how he feel, huh. On my way out, Mr. Tourney come bustin in yellin, One of you idiots put the microwave and Xerox on at the same time and the smartboard shut off in the middle of my lesson.

Long time ago, Swan's father and me was arguin because some woman gave him a bunch of balloons for his birthday, and I said that was flirtin and he said, No, it wasn't flirtin. It turned heated and I said suttin else he was not ready to hear and he drop-kicked me in the stomach area and I lost my wind. So I stopped lovin him at night. For a whole year he snuggled me and rubbed me, did his nose like this on my shoulder and said, Baby, baby, baby, let's try one time, but I said, No, thank you, next time you'll think twice about usin karate on people you supposedly care about.

My job at the airport is simple. I stand at the scanner before the departure gates and make sure people take they shoes off. I got an answer for everything. You're gonna make me miss my plane. Next time, leave the house accountin for this. All our electronics have to go in the bin? Only the ones you don't want to beep. I've been in this line for an hour. And you'll be on the beach for weeks.

Today, this girl said, That's it. I've had it with all these cocka-
mamie security checks. It's always the young white ones throwin
tantrums as if someone couldn't just up and decide to knock they
skinny ass out. One guy answered her, said, So people like me
don't blow the whole place up. Everybody in the line turned and
it was a young guy in one of them long Muslim dresses. It was one
of them things where you had to crack up, even considerin the
situation and what have you. That kept me goin for a few hours.
Of course my boss didn't think it was funny and pulled me aside
talkin bout, Let's give him a real thorough pat down just in case.

It's Friday, so I treat myself and eat at the restaurant over by
Gate C. I order suttin good with steak in it. You spend all your
time watchin people heftin around carry-ons and sayin things of
importance to people while they lookin at they cell phones and to
be frank, you wanna be like them. Some of my days off, I come
anyway, in plainclothes and buy a box of encased cigars, or I'll buy
a pair of expensive headphones out the vendin machine for Swan.

While I watch two stewardesses outside the restaurant roll
they luggage and three kids tryna run the opposite way of the
movin sidewalk when they should know better, I count my total
hours for the week and my projected pay minus the taxes. I make
sure to add the four hours of Adalis's shift when she left early to
celebrate her birthday. I do forty-four, that's the hours I work,
times ten dollars, my hourly wage—it's really fourteen, but again
minus the taxes. It's a lot considerin it wasn't no time-and-a-half
this week, but not enough. I cut into my steak knowin that for
twenty minutes nobody can say jack-diddly about where I have to
be. I start daydreamin about what if I was an air traffic controller
or even one of the information representatives. They can make

up to twenty-five an hour sittin behind a desk, restin they feet. I must of been daydreamin for twenty-one minutes, because I wake to my name bein paged.

There's a faculty and staff meetin that Monday before they send us off on Christmas break and Ms. Chalmers is mad and nervous. She was wearin a gray business suit and red pumps in the mornin and now she's in a blouse and sneakers. It's way different from when she be in her office writin me up, holdin a cup of coffee like she holdin a cup of liquid power. I wanna find some kinda solace in that, except this look like suttin else.

As you know our school's been on the watchlist this past year, she start. Sometimes they observe you at the wrong time, and all of a sudden, that's the snapshot of your school that stays forever.

A couple of teachers cough. The paras, we all sittin together lookin around like, I hope y'all know we not the reason we in this mess. Meanwhile, Mr. Broderick sittin there twiddlin his thumbs, can't look me in the eye and I don't know why.

Chalmers go, I received an email from the office of the superintendent a few days ago saying that our quality review is set for some time in April. I repeat, some time. They didn't say what exact day it was gonna be, because it's my understanding that it will be a surprise.

All the rustlin and chair-creakin stop.

Ms. Chalmers keeps on.

Yes, the superintendent of the district will email me *twenty-four hours* in advance, and we'll have exactly that amount of time to fit together all these moving pieces.

Mr. Tourney, the math teacher who been rottin here for years, raise his hand.

Why'd they choose this year to start this rubbish, he say, standin up and squeezin his eyebrows so that everybody could see. I've been teaching in this school since the beginning of the Clinton years, when they actually let you teach, and it was either you were doing a satisfactory job or not. If they *were* pulling something like this, they'd have the decency to give you a few months' notice.

Usually don't nobody side with Mr. Tourney because his face is covered with all these hair dots since he don't like shavin, but this meetin everybody else arms is folded, too.

Ms. Chalmers, bein that she grew up not too far from here, in Spanish Harlem, and know how to keep her tongue sharp, go, Let me remind you that we dragged ourselves into this. We sat back and allowed the students to use the laptops to go on porno sites. We let Rhiann's mother come in to fight a seventh grader. We were showing them episodes of *Seinfeld* instead of teaching them how to balance equations. Last year the reviewer asked Kimberly, one of our brightest, to show them a piece of graded work, and do you know what she said? She said, they don't grade our work, they only give us grades on our report cards.

She was throwin a lot of shade in Mr. Tourney's direction seein how apparently Mr. Tourney did a lot of that stuff, but she wasn't gonna name no names cuz she didn't have to. She went on about how she cherished her job and how she took the 4 train and put herself thru grad school with two small children who used to pee on themselves in the class sometimes. She said her kids be cryin to be with they dad who is a police officer upstate, but she know she made a sacrifice keepin them near the school, and she intend to stick to it. Left the speech right there and said there was eggnog and pie in the back corner of the library if we cared for it.

Ms. Dallas, she say, tappin me on the shoulder on the way out. Can I speak to you?

In the hallway, next to the owls the eighth graders drew for they science project and the paragraphs the sixth graders wrote about some empire, Ms. Chalmers go, Mr. Broderick has been telling me that you're undermining his authority in the classroom. That you're encouraging students to do the opposite of what he says. Do you care to respond to that?

No, I say.

Why not? she say.

Because I see he ain't tell you the whole part of the story, I say.

You want to share your side of the story?

If I told her I was tryna keep her friggin school from fallin apart, then I'd be wrong. So I only say, I can't say I do.

Well, consider yourself verbally warned, she say.

It's the end of January and we ain't have school Monday or Tuesday cuz of snow days they had to twist Bloomberg's arm to give us. Should of seen the snow up to the custodian's clavicle. They had to go and suspend 3 train service and the only way kids could make it here was by the crosstown buses. Wednesday we opened late and it was still up to they waist and all you seen was kids floatin on top of it and teachers gettin pelt with snowballs and not knowin where they came from.

The kids have lost it and that ain't by no fault of my own.

Today, Trayson come in wavin his hands in the air, singin Back, back that ass up. Deja come in stickin bubblegum in Kimberly hair and Kimberly turn around and go, Stop it! Raven come in smellin like perfume. Arnaud come in smellin like shit. Franchesca Jimenez come in talkin Spanglish. Lashaun, aka Kowboy, come in swingin his book bag at fat Najee. The rest come in textin, coughin, spittin, and kissin.

Now they on Shakespeare in Mr. Broderick's class. They readin that one with all the fairies runnin thru the forest sprinklin love juice on each other. Mr. Broderick tell the kids it's a comedy and that mean everybody gonna be hitched up by the end of it, but to me there's nothin funny about people gettin married. If anything, it's serious and involve cryin.

Who would like to read Puck? Mr. Broderick ask.

Me, me, me, Kimberly say.

All right, Kimberly is Puck, he say. Who would like to read Titania?

When no one else raise they hand, Kimberly say me, me, me again.

You already have Puck's lines.

I can handle two parts.

Fine.

Kimberly, who think she some kinda spellin bee champ, raise her hand to read Lysander, Demetrius, and Helena, but Mr. Broderick, he go ahead and nix her and substitute some roles for hisself cuz he said he was a thespian in high school and everybody should have some good Shakespeare under they belt. He go ahead and pick Cassius to read, too, tryna show me he a great teacher, but everybody know Cassius read one word every five minutes and the teacher usually gotta stand over his shoulder and say, The, and he say, The, and then, Frog, and he say, Frog, and then, Jumped, and he say, Jumped. So I'm flippin thru one of the Shakespeare books and I go, Mr. Broderick, Imma help him out. And Mr. Broderick go, I would like to see him practice on his own, thank you very much. I go, Now doin that would be plain old— I stop myself. If it wasn't for Ms. Chalmers and her verbal warnins, I would have said plain old stupid.

Kimberly there pronouncin her thines and thous. She all into herself like she need to be smacked back down. Meanwhile Mr. Broderick start waxin off on how this play is all about how the father wouldn't let the daughter marry who she wanted so she had to sneak behind his back. And for a second I wish I went to school like Mr. Broderick instead of hangin around Harlem goin la-la-la. The kids don't understand a word he sayin except they know he sayin suttin smart. Ay Dawan raise his hand and go, Mr. Broderick, you went to Harvard right, and Mr. Broderick go, Sure did, and Ay Dawan scratch his temple like he tryna figure suttin out. The rest of the class is like, What, what, Ay Dawan, just ask your damn question and stop scratchin your damn head, you idiot. And finally he go, Mr. Broderick, if you went to Harvard, how come you not somewhere makin a million dollars on a spaceship somewhere? Then it's like somebody pressed the shush button and the rest of the class go quiet.

Mr. Broderick say, Because, because—and before he give one of them typical answers about helpin people and givin back, I see his Adam's apple rise up in his neck like an elevator, and realize Ay Dawan went somewhere he wasn't supposed to go.

.　.　.

Kandese been awful quiet the past two weeks. She not Ay Dawan or Najee or Kowboy or Shequanna Flowers who just was safety transferred cuz she got punched in the mouth for bein too much of a damn busybody. Kandese like her jeans tight up against her butt and the Jordans too big for her feet, but other than that she her own self. She not no presidential scholar or nothin like that, but she can be smart when she want to. Ms. Chalmers came up with the bright idea of makin the kids take economics when 99 percent of them still tap they fingers to they mouth when they add, but the way Kandese was askin questions about business models and things like that—I said it's a shame that teacher quit and went back to Wall Street. The only time Kandese name was caught up in anything was the day after Field Day, when everybody had time to go frolickin in the grass, but nobody had time to do they homework. Mr. Tourney was readin everybody grades out loud as examples of a slovenly attitude. He come to Kandese and Kandese was like, Don't read my grades out loud. Mr. Tourney said, You should of thought of that before the integers quiz you didn't study for—sixty-five, sixty, sixty. And Kandese stood up like, I said *don't* read my grades out loud. Took the stapler on his desk and broke it in half against the door. Tiny, tiny, girl like that. The class turnt so serious til Kowboy said, That's that mama-grab-the-skillet strength, and Najee said, Yeah, that's that slow-boy-don't-pick-on-me strength.

But like I said, Kandese been awful quiet lately, and these past four days she ain't even make it to school. She live at Banneker Terrace not too far down from me so this Saturday I decide to ask around and do my due diligence. She live downstairs in 3A. I know she live with her father and the only thing I know about him is he really old and really fat. I knock on the door for ten whole minutes and I say to myself, Two and two don't add up.

The tenant association old ladies is in the bingo room spreadin gossip when I poke my head and interrupt. They have a runnin Rolodex of everybody and everything goin on.

Excuse me, I say. Anybody by chance know what's with Kandese in 3A, she ain't been in school awhile.

Corinthia—she has glaucoma in her right eye so bad it open up all the way and she can't shut it—she go, If you came to the tenant meetins, you would know.

And I go, I woulda told you if I came down for a finger waggin.

Corinthia stand up immediately and go, Don't you come down here and talk to me like that.

And I say to the other ladies, Hold her because she sound like she wanna get taught suttin real quick.

And Quanneisha, the only nice one, whisper to Corinthia, Just tell her.

And Corinthia go, Fine. That girl and her father are in a shelter now—renovation hike was too much. But you don't have to worry bout that, Ms. Verona Dallas. What you providin for: family of three, right? Don't worry. When you in enough arrears, they'll prolly shove you into a one-bedroom. Your son will have the livin room and you and your daughter will share the bed.

That night I go to my envelopes. I rub all the bills I done stored over the years. I don't trust Citibank after I learnt they was seepin money out my account just for nothin. It total up to $1,500. I sigh because with this new bump for renovations I'll be lucky if this last me til June. Juju work at Forever 21 before she go to night classes. She slide me a few dollars, but I feel guilty takin them. I sit there in my room by myself thinkin nobody know my worries, nobody but me and God.

Later in the week, Swan knock durin *So You Think You Can Dance*.

I found myself a job, he say.

Doin what?

They got me wearin a chicken suit in front of this restaurant in Times Square. It's me and two Mexican ladies dressed up as turkeys. They cool, Ma. They teachin me Spanish.

He slapped five damp twenties down on my nightstand. I picked them up and put them in my purse.

Thank you, I say.

You welcome, Mama.

But quit that job.

But, Ma—

Call them and tell them tomorrow's your last day.

Teachers talk behind each other's back so much it's funny. I'm in the lounge heatin up pasta salad cuz that's how I like it, and they cracklin over the computer cuz they found Mr. Nabisko's datin profile sayin he wears emeralds in his heart. Soon as Mr. Broderick leave for his next class, all of a sudden it's his turn to be the ass of the jokes. I find out his father some kind of rich inventor who cooked up some piece that go in all telescopes. They be interviewin him on PBS sometimes. You should see them, all the twenty-suttin-year-old teachers, leanin on the file cabinets like they around a campfire.

One of the girls, I forget her name, she be in the lab all day, she go, I don't get it, his father's a world-famous engineer, he went to Harvard, and the only place he could find a job was here?

Another one of them, Mr. G, he start chucklin and go, Then he spends his whole day lecturing all of us on how smart he is. I hope he doesn't do that in his classes. That's a sure recipe for being eaten up.

Another say, Is he gonna do this forever?

And another say, Waste of a degree.

By the time my salad done finished in the microwave, I can't help my nosy self. I find out Mr. Broderick told Ms. Botelli he wanna work here a couple of years and make enough money to travel the globe. He gonna start off in Australia and see if he can get hisself to every continent.

Ms. Botelli go, I hear behavior in his class is a mess, and Ms. Chalmers is startin to get wind of it.

There's a part in that *Midsummer* Shakespeare play where one of the fairies is talkin trash about hisself. Think of it like a rap, Mr. Broderick tell the class, but that's the furthest thing it is from in my opinion. He assign Cassius a role again and his readin sound like somebody's stalled carburetor. "Thou . . . speakst . . . aright," and even Kimberly looks like she bout to pluck her own eyes out. My mind is out the window with the bare trees on the sidewalk and the two security guards eatin pierogies. I'm hopin, even though it's February and I had enough of this weather, that it'll snow one more day, and they'll cancel. I'll still get paid here, and I can do a double shift at JFK. I come to and Cassius is lookin up from the page with his finger on only the second line and he say to Mr. Broderick, Can I start over?

Out the blue, Kowboy pull two gold Magnum condoms out his bag. Mr. Broderick don't see what it is and he go, Lashaun, turn around and pay attention, please. When Mr. Broderick ain't lookin, Kowboy go, These is for my girls. The class bust out cracklin. I bust out cracklin, too, not cuz what he say is funny but cuz I'm imaginin him fittin his tiny wee-wee in that potato sack and gettin all tangled up. I can't control myself and Mr. Broderick shoot a look at me like I have the mind of a child.

Kowboy stand up for me and go, What, it's just condoms, you seen these before, right? And then he turn to the class and say, You know Mr. Broderick be all up in some pussy. He the type to be all up in it and start cryin, like, You're so pretty, this is the best pussy I ever had.

The class is dyin and, at this moment, Kowboy is throwin his condoms in the air and catchin them and Najee, he wanna do everything Kowboy do. He take his condoms, the cheap ones they keep in a tin bucket in front of the nurse's office, and start throwin his up in the air like tiny Frisbees. Mr. Broderick is like, You two, stop it, that's inappropriate. He tryna make his teeth block all the anger in his voice, but all that do is make everybody laugh louder except for Kandese. Her head been down the whole period. Somebody should check if she dead. Everybody laughin, laughin, then Najee throw his condom. It land on top one of the big lights and don't come down.

Mr. Broderick go, That's it, I'm phoning the office.

Kowboy go, See what you get for tryna be me.

Najee go, No, Mr. Broderick, no, Imma get it down.

Mr. Broderick sulk. Najee zip open his bag and take out one of his Nike sneakers.

I have good aim. Watch.

Before Mr. Broderick or anybody can stop him, he fling the shoe at the condom. It look like it's about to work until it hit the light and the casin come crashin down. The class go, *Oooh*, except Kandese, who wake up for one second, dig her nose, and bury her head back down. And that's when Mr. Broderick look at me all furious.

Can you believe Mr. Broderick have the nerve to cast his shade in my direction like I started all that?

February came and went with nothin much except the bondage they had on stage for the Black history play. Now it's March and I'm stayin away from trouble. I been skippin Mr. Broderick class for the whole week because I can't right now, I just can't. I make sure he don't see me in the mornin when the seventh graders come thru the annex, and I hide in the teacher lounge bathroom fifth period, but this don't last long. This fool Ay Dawan done brought handcuffs to school and handcuffed Cassius to the desk. Everybody yellin and trippin over themselves. The custodian had to come with the jaws of life. Where is his para? Mr. Broderick yell. Where is his para? Ms. Chalmers herself come bargin in the bathroom while I'm holdin a mascara brush in front of the mirror.

Now I'm in Ms. Chalmers office again bein chided like so many times before, except the big difference is now I'm sittin next to Mr. Broderick.

Whatever's going on between you two, she say, her eyebrows lookin like two black roaches with tangled-up antennas, it needs to end right now.

We sittin in front of her like two children in time-out. I don't want to look at either her or him so the only thing my eye can land on is the diploma Ms. Chalmers hung up on the wall.

I got the rest of the period, so one of you speak up.

Mr. Broderick take his cue and start spillin out everything.

He go, It's Ms. Dallas. She's immature and sophomoric and a general ulcer.

Ms. Chalmers go, You're tossing a lot of words in the air.

And Mr. Broderick go, She's the reason that fifth period is total chaos. She's either inciting a riot or watching it from the sidelines.

Ms. Dallas, what do you have to say to that?

What I have to say is his class is chaos because he don't know how to teach.

Now the gloves is off both of us. Mr. Broderick go, She antagonizes students and then she laughs at their lewd jokes. She's a general malaise.

I go, Ms. Chalmers, I'm Black, right?

Mr. Broderick go, This has nothing to do with race and everything to do with a lack of professionalism.

I go, Really? Tell me, Mr. Broderick, what you'll be doin in three years from now. Imma still be here. You'll be travelin the world usin your daddy's American Express. Don't think I don't know.

He go, Whatever will cast the spotlight away from your incompetence, huh?

Ms. Chalmers clap her hands on her desk so hard a tiny bit of cold coffee spill out her thermos.

Listen to yourselves! she yell.

Find a way to make it work, Ms. Chalmers end up sayin, so I did. I didn't say nothin to the man from then on. Cassius say, Ms. Dallas, I need one of them worksheets about forceful verbs, and I go, Ask Mr. Broderick your damn self and learn some responsibility. Closest me and Mr. Broderick come to communication was gruntin. None of the little ones notice except for Ay Dawan, who asked me in front of some of his friends, Do you like Mr. Broderick? and I said, I work with everybody I have to. He go, I'll take that as a no.

This arrangement was fine. The students was doin desk beats every minute and hangin off the ceilin. Ain't no learnin goin on, but admin was off our back. The spring dance came. I was a chaperone and I was flashin light on the boys and sayin, What's that inside your jacket and I would find out it was the girl they was dancin with's booty.

They called me in for a meetin with a buildin representative. I knew what it was about, but Swan and Juju, who was there, too, couldn't have had the farthest clue. I should have responded to the letters management sent me, but nothin short of me puttin actual money in the rent envelope would of changed anything. We three there in a classroom, and it's a Black lady with a pointer and a whiteboard talkin bout, You have the one-bedroom option or there's also the studio option, as if all of us could fit into either.

Shoulda seen Swan. Like he was some CEO in some boardroom talkin bout, What does this mean, what does this mean? I was proud and aggravated cuz now he wanna be concerned about our finances? I also wished the Black lady would stop frontin like she was givin us a choice.

We moved into a one-bedroom three floors down from our old apartment. They was Scotch tape on the walls and stains in the corner. The outlet in the livin room was out and all you see is all these wires. Me and Juju take the one bedroom cuz of the private things we women have to do, and Swan took the livin room. I thought about us havin company over and them seein a pair of Swan's boxers on the floor out the corner of they eye.

Our first night, Juju is textin, and I'm dottin my face. In bed Juju see suttin on her phone screen and keep hidin her laugh and sayin, Oh no they didn't, Oh no they didn't. She put her hand to her mouth, see me silent on the other side of the bed with my hands folded in my lap. She say, Oh I guess it's time to go to sleep now. We spent the whole night turnin and whisperin, You got enough covers and pullin the sheets from each other. I woke in the mornin with a crick in my neck.

From the time I reach the school it's just static all around. People bumpin into me and people stutterin. I'm like, This is finally the day when the whole world has gone crazy. Then I hear the whispers: The superintendent is comin. They sent Ms. Chalmers the email. Said tomorrow morning at eight, Happy Easter. Boy, is people scramblin. Off the bat, second period me and Cassius notice Mr. Tourney done already stashed away the nail clippers and shavers he always leave on the corner of his desk. On the way to third period, the custodian is sweepin up mouse droppins that's been in the hallway since I don't know when. Teachers is everywhere stuffin everything in closets. In the lounge, everybody voice is shiverin. They not playin hangman on the computer. All you hear besides the shiverin is printin and staplin.

The only two who ain't really fazed is Ms. Botelli and Mr. Nyim who, in my opinion, is the best teachers. They talkin to each other because the good teachers have no time for nobody else.

Mr. Nyim go, I don't know what all this hullabaloo is about. This is the year they shut the school down. It's a foregone conclusion.

Ms. Botelli go, Absolutely, nothing has changed. No consequences for misbehavior, nothing.

Mr. Nyim go, I've sent résumés out. Between you and me, this is my last year either way.

Ms. Botelli go, Wow.

I like Mr. Nyim cuz he be usin words like hullabaloo.

Another period, Ms. Paisley, the blond who teach science, is talkin to Ms. Withermeyer, the social studies teacher, and she like, God, I hope they don't visit my fourth period tomorrow. Then Ms. Withermeyer say, I'm gonna just teach my best lesson, and if they're acting like animals around me, so be it. Who I feel bad for is Broderick.

·   ·   ·

Right before fifth period, guess who gonna corner me.

I hope you aren't worried about the superintendent visit tomorrow, Mr. Broderick say. Behind him Ay Dawan at the water fountain pretendin he lickin the water all seductive.

I wanna be like, Hell yeah, I'm worried. I'm goddamn near fifty. I can't up and relocate over *your* foolishness.

But instead I say, I guess the only thing we can do is cross our heart and see.

But he smilin like nothin devised can take his joy away.

I'm takin a grad class that's changin my life, he say. With a few adjustments, I have a feelin things are gonna be A-OK again. We're going to get a handle on this situation, he say, like we teammates.

He basically tell me that in night school he readin this wonderful book called *Suttin, Suttin of the Oppressed*. That in the book it said that people don't value school if they don't first know they poor. If they know they poor, then they gonna hustle about they education to pull theyselves up. He say all this as the students is walkin into class and slammin books and takin out they Arizona bottles. He also say these theories go great with *A Raisin in the Sun*, cuz one of the characters, Walter Lee, is aware of all this, and that's what make him different. And I go, Worth a try, but deep down I'm with Ms. Withermeyer when she say this ship done already sunk.

Mr. Broderick begin, I'd like to continue our discussion of this classic play by examining Walter Lee. He tell everyone the page to turn to and then rub his lips like we all bout to get our appetite whetted. The class is serious. You would think it was college for a minute, but then the radiator go *urr*—ur, ur, *urr*—and the class start dyin.

To Ay Dawan, who got his head on the desk hynoptizin hisself with his pencil, Mr. Broderick say, Ay Dawan, what can you tell us about Walter Lee?

He raise his head and go, He a idiot, then put his head back down. The class start rollin again. Some of them can't laugh normal, I swear. Sound like lawn mowers.

Fair enough, Mr. Broderick say with his eye on me. But can you tell us why you think that?

I don't know. Leave me alone.

Because I happen to disagree. In fact, I think you're 100 percent wrong.

This is a new kinda thing for Mr. Broderick to say, and almost everybody prick up they ears, even Ay Dawan. And I'll tell you why you're wrong, Broderick continue, why you're so very wrong, but you'll have to promise me you'll listen. Can you listen, just once? Walter Lee is like all the people in our country who go to work pumping gas or working a cash register, but for this difference: he may be sadder than everybody else, but he's better off, because he knows he's poor and he's trying to do something about it. Like we all should.

That's when Kowboy start singin, She lick, lick me like a lollipop. That get everybody uproarin again.

Lashaun, Mr. Broderick say, that was low.

And Kowboy go, Wait, wait, wait, mister. What you mean by we all should?

Mr. Broderick kick his feet up on the desk until some of the girls in the front row notice the thread comin off one of his sneakers and start pointin, so he cock his feet back down. He so pleased with hisself. He think he went zoop zoop and caught them all with his fishin pole. Cassius's teeth is ready to jut on out his mouth, but I close his jaw for him cuz I wanna see how this man's gonna flip this for these ghetto boys and girls.

He go, All I'm sayin is it's good for us to know our place in the world.

With full stank, the two girls in front go, What are you tryna say?

I'm saying, Mr. Broderick go. What am I saying? What I'm saying is let's take a poll. Right now. It's simple. Think about where you belong in the world and raise your hand accordingly. Here are the three options: rich, poor, or middle. So: How many of you consider yourselves poor?

I inhale, givin myself away, cuz I know all the ones that raise they hand is like me. But only three of them do.

Okay, Mr. Broderick go, not expectin that. Well, how many of you consider yourselves in the middle?

All the ones who shoulda raised they hand for poor raise they hand, but still not everybody.

How many consider themselves rich?

Like ten of them raise they hand, and one of them is Kowboy, of course, and Mr. Broderick, he disgusted cuz the opposite of his plan is what's happenin. I wanna crack a smile but I say to myself, Let me not before I give Ms. Chalmers more fuel for her fire.

Mr. Broderick go, All right, those people who raised their hands. Can any of you explain to me how you are rich?

Najee stand up and blurt out, My mama is an entrepreneur. She own her own daycare.

Mr. Broderick, he exhale out loud and go, I didn't call on you.

Then he take like a Buddhist second or suttin to calm down and then go, Lashaun, what about you? Why are you rich?

Kowboy shrug his shoulders and go, I don't know. Cuz my mother buy whatever I want.

Like what?

I don't know—like expensive shit.

Expensive stuff like what? Come on now, you know the rule: be specific.

I don't know, mister—like an iPad.

Okay, that's nice. What about pricier things, like computers?

Ain't an iPad a computer?

I mean like a laptop.

Yeah, she can buy me that as long as I ask her early so she can put in for overtime at her job.

What about a European vacation? Can she buy you a European vacation?

I don't wanna go to Europe.

Then Kowboy realize what Mr. Broderick tryna do and he shut himself down and go, Mister, I don't have to explain nothin to you, I—

But Mr. Broderick go, What about a house? Can she buy you a house? Or a plane? Then he smile cuz he feel like he got Kowboy right where he want him.

Kowboy go, You tryna play me.

I'm not trying to play you—I'm trying to make a point. Can she? Answer the question.

Kowboy's face just turn into a pair of curtains, the heavy drapes kind. He take a deep breath, and it's like the curtains is comin down.

Then he lift his head and start singin, I'm just a small-town girl, livin in a lonely world.

Twenty-nine voices at the same time bust out laughin, and Mr. Broderick is tryna hush em all. He look at Kowboy like he could destroy his face.

Kowboy go, What? It's just song lyrics.

Then he sing, I took the midnight train goin anywhere.

Then Najee pop out and go, We built this city. We built this city on rock and roll.

And the rest of the students is singin, some of them leanin back in they seats, enjoyin the show. You start to see Arizona bottles twisted open and sipped up. There's a punch one goin round and people is drinkin it and squintin they eyes and I was thinkin, These nasty kids can't even drink from they own bottle. The whole time Mr. Broderick is yelpin, yelpin, and everybody is goin about they conversations while he over there dyin on the side of the road.

Mr. Broderick go, I guess nobody wants to learn today?

Some people give him little bits of attention, but that's as far as it goes.

Mr. Broderick continue, Walter Lee wouldn't raise his hand and say he was rich, I'll tell you that much.

Kimberly, the only one who been readin the book, raise her hand and say, Mister, I know you not talkin about me. I live with my mother and my aunt in the George Washington Houses and we have a TV in every room, thank you very much.

Everybody go, Ooh, and Ay Dawan get squeaky and go, Get him, Kimberly. Tell him to bring that ass right here.

Kowboy unzip his school bag and out come a radio this big like the one my older brother used to have in the eighties before he started spendin his money on vials. He turn the volume all the way up so the bass is goin *boom boom boom*. The voice is sayin, You're a jerk, You're a jerk. Then all of a sudden you see Mookie, who I thought had some sense, jump into the aisle and start dancin—and he can really dance. The rest of everybody knock over the desks and form a circle. Cassius, too, before I could yank his shirt. All of them, clappin and goin, Ahh, ahh, ahh.

Shoulda seen Mr. Broderick turn red. It start from his neck like soda foam and before you know it, he there eruptin. He open the classroom door. Ms. Chalmers, Ms. Chalmers! he scream and two nosy teachers from across the hall peek out they windows. Sure as butter, here come Ms. Chalmers cloppin over. All you see is kids dashin back to they desks, but they not foolin nobody cuz the desks ain't in rows.

Really, Ms. Chalmers say, not tryna control the Rs she rollin. The day before the school visit?

Mr. Broderick nod his head like he acceptin some kind of victory. Who was involved?

Mr. Broderick point out Mookie, Najee, and Kowboy and they shove they desks in front of them all aggressive, and Kowboy go to Mr. Broderick and say, You's a liar on everything I love. Najee go, I wish I had Mr. Nyim instead of you. Ms. Chalmers is draggin Kowboy while he keep sayin, I swear, I swear. The crazy thing is that all this took eight minutes. I'm peerin up at the clock hopin the bell is gonna ring soon and stop all this dead in its tracks. When it does I walk out the classroom with Cassius, my whole demeanor saggin down to the ground. One of the girls tap me on the shoulder and go, Miss, miss, miss, and I go, What, and she go, They was sippin Cîroc in that Arizona bottle.

·   ·   ·

That Tuesday, Mr. Wallace, Kandese father, died. They foundt him in the livin room of their unit at the shelter with eyes wide open, stiff as a rooster, naked with his hand in his crotch. Said Kandese moved the hand out, slid boxers on him, and called 911 like it was another day in the park. Tenant ladies said when they got there, the fumes in the carpet smelled worse than the body.

I'm in my buildin's management office tryna finally get hold of a spare entrance key for Swan when I see Kandese in one of the seats eatin a bag of hot cheese popcorn and fillin out papers. Her hair is tied up in a ponytail and a pink barrette. Most likely did it without a mirror. Her jaw is serious. When I look deep in her eye ducts, there's crud all in em.

Kandese, I say. Sorry about your father.

And she say, Thank you, miss.

And I say, What they have you up here doin?

And she say, The other place need to know something about my last address so they can see where I'm gonna go.

You don't have nobody to take care of you?

I'm sposed to maybe stay with my aunt in Brooklyn a few days, but she said she got her hands tied. I might have to go down south to my grandmother's.

Where you stayin until then?

The shelter.

By yourself?

Yeah.

In the same place your father died?

Yeah.

I don't wanna hear anymore, so I tap on the secretary desk and say, Where's Jabari? How come Jabari's everywhere but in the damn office?

Then I turn to Kandese and be like, I understand if I don't see you for a few days at the school.

As soon as I open the top lock to my own place, Swan come bombardin me with pleadin eyes. He holdin a clear recyclin bag with clothes in it.

I say, Swan, baby, what's the matter, even though the only matter I care about is my feet findin a place to rest.

Swan dangle the bag in my face, Can't you see? It's Juju messin with my underwear.

Then Juju pop out from behind the corner wall like she was only waitin for Swan to draw first blood.

She go, Ma, he has to be mindful that he is sleepin in the livin room.

Swan go, And that's why you took all my drawers and left them on the counter for everybody?

Better that than splayed over the floor.

Swan go, Stop treatin me like an animal. I'm not no animal.

Juju's mouth's runnin like she ain't blink to consider what Swan said, so he turn to me and say, Ma, please tell her this ain't no Forever 21 and she can't be bossin people around.

He have a point about that. That's suttin I been observin about Juju ever since they up and made her a floor manager.

Juju, with her hands in a steeple, go, Ma, tell Swan we both tired of payin to be his hotel worker.

Swan go, That's how you feel? Then don't eat or use my stuff no more, *comprende*?

He march right past Juju, makin sure she feel his wind, open up the refrigerator and take out the fluffernutter, some leftover macaroni he made, plus the microwave bean burritos out the freezer, and then he go near the stove top and rip his George Foreman out the outlet. He bring all that stuff to the small table and wrap his arms around it all and his chin, too.

Juju give him the sorriest look.

Oh please, she say.

She say that right around the time I decide to step into the kitchen and sit down at the table next to both of them.

I wait for them to quit and notice me.

Come this time next year, I say, I'm not gonna have a job. Then the whole thing about tomorrow's school visit and what's been goin on in Mr. Broderick's class come pourin out like sweet rain.

And all Juju can do is nod. All Swan can do is unwrap his arms from around his stuff and listen.

Usually this early the school's main office door is locked tight, with the lights cut off. You be tryna jiggle it so you can go in and punch your time card, but this mornin it is buzzin with bees. The gym teacher is in there collectin his folder and he wearin a suit. I don't see his whistle nowhere. Right next door, in the Save Room, Kowboy, Najee, and twenty of the baddest kids in the school is holed up in there before class. They all reachin out to me like, Miss, miss, why they have us holed up, school ain't even start. We ain't even had the chance to do nothin yet. Ms. Chalmers with her red pumps come barkin at the AP. Why are all of them in there like that? AP shrug his shoulders. I figured you wanted certain students out of the classrooms today. Ms. Chalmers bark on him like, We did that last year, remember, and they found them and wrote us up.

I notice the AP has on a brand-new suit, too, that the air around me smell like perfume and cologne, and I seem to be the only one who came in my usual Wednesday attire, which is my jean dress that I swiped on sale two years ago at T.J. Maxx before anyone else could.

Ms. Chalmers disappear down the hall and poof, poof she reappear with the superintendent, and all me and the two teachers beside me can think is, There she is, there she is. They send someone different every year, but this woman give off the feelin of you-seen-her-before. The type of white woman that, no matter what school you escape from, will track you down and scribble down notes on every mistake you makin so as to make it permanent. By her business suit alone, lighter than navy blue with the white ruffles fluffin out from her blouse and pantyhose tight on those ham hocks of hers, I know for a fact she ain't from the city. No way you ride the subway every day with no wear-down on that fabric. I know for a fact she one of those big boss ladies who live all the way upstate in a *house* house cookin Pillsbury dough for her kids in the evenin, then wakin up in the mornin to drive to Harlem and give everybody hell. I know that cuz her face look like the Pillsbury dough she cook.

Ms. Chalmers and the lady walk by me, and Ms. Chalmers say to the lady, There goes one of our most esteemed paras. I say, Mornin, and the lady put out her hand all limp without sayin anything. When they leave I whisper to myself, Let the fakeness begin.

As far as I know, this is what happens. The superintendent meet with the principal in the mornin with the door closed. The principal go, I want you to see this, this, and this class, aka, the ones that's gonna make me look good. The superintendent go, We only seein one of those classes plus this and this class, aka, the ones you might be hidin secrets in. All the while you a teacher, you a para, and you don't know if/when they gonna duck in and start writin down stuff about you. I swear the whole day is watchin your back and not bein able to sit straight in a chair.

I peek into Ms. Botelli room, and she on her hands and knees, dustin off under her desk. She doin that and her eyelids is up at the clock cuz any minute the bell gonna ring and a flood of sixth graders gonna come kickin thru the door. Get up off the floor, Ms. Botelli, I want to say. This whole school is damned. The bell that sound like a fire alarm, the clouded-up fountains, the wall paint from nineteen-freakin-fifteen, pardon my French, all of it. People who never set one foot in this place know it ain't much. I was two hours outside Louisville one summer because someone told me you could taste the original Kentucky chicken there, and this person I met said to me, You work at Sojourner Truth Middle? Geez Louise.

I know if I was Sojourner Truth or Martin Luther King or whoever it may be restin in southern soil, I would not be restin peacefully. Shoot, if I was them, I would come back as a ghost in the walls and haunt folks. I'd be like, You think you honorin me with these cruddy buildins? Think again. If I was Sojourner

Truth, I'd take one look at this school and be like, You might as well have named a slave ship after me.

Anyways, I'm seein mishaps everywhere. In the hallway, between period two and three, Kowboy jump while Mookie is under the Sojourner Truth banner and say, Kowboy elevates for the dunk and his dick is in Mookie's mouth, ready to nut! And right around the corner come the principal and the superintendent. Everybody is wonderin if she heard it and is writin it down.

Third and fourth period, I'm beside Cassius, bitin my nails. If they gonna come, let them come now, cuz if they come durin fifth period, whoo, boy, I say to myself, and Cassius have the nerve to eye me like I'm the one who need services. Then I ask myself why I care so much, since I been preachin all this time that the school was goin caput.

Bing, bing, fifth. Of all things this fool Broderick choose to wear, he pick a white dress shirt. Anytime he raise his hand, that sweat splotch is blam, right there for all. We file in and it's like a regular day in Chaosville. Kimberly is carryin a bottle of chocolate Yoo-hoo, and somebody, I think it was one of the African boys, turn around and accidentally knock it over with his book bag. Chocolate milk spilt on the floor, and Kimberly go, I'm not cleanin that up, and the African boy go, I'm not cleanin that up either. That's nasty, and Kimberly go, You shouldn't have a problem. Don't y'all live like that back home, and Mr. Broderick go, Hey, hey, hey, we don't talk like that, and Najee go, Ooh, ooh, ooh, lemme get some paper towels, and Mr. Broderick go, Fine, and Najee bring the paper towels and just heave it on the milk and leave it there to sop up and stick to the ground.

Mr. Broderick is tryna settle everybody down. I feel his vibe toward me like, Why ain't you settlin them down, too, and I play the fool.

Guys, I need you to behave, Mr. Broderick say, and while the desks is screechin and topplin over, he add, We might have an important visitor today.

Ay Dawan hear him and go, Fuck a visitor. If she was here now, I'd be like—he run off to the computer cart by the chalkboard and start humpin it. Each time he act like the computer cart is so big it's blowin him up. The picture of tiny-ass Ay Dawan humpin suttin three times his size is too much for the class, and now no one can shut up. After he finish his show, he sit back down. Two students give him five on his way back to his desk, which make his face all shiny and greasy.

Spin the globe and land your finger on any classroom in the world and this right here will still be the worst. But the good news is, it's already fifteen minutes in and that door ain't cracked open since Najee run to the bathroom. Maybe they won't visit. Maybe they went to all the good classes. Maybe the lady stamped her clipboard and renewed our school already.

No sooner do that dream finish gettin dreamt do the hinge squeak open and there go the principal, the AP, and the superintendent lady comin in like pallbearers. Right off the bat the lady get her heels stuck in the chocolate and paper towel mess on the floor. Ms. Chalmers is there thinkin should she help or just stand there and look professional.

Mr. Broderick see them, and he immediately act like everything's under control.

All right, boys and girls, Mr. Broderick go. Open your books to Act III.

His voice is shakin all over itself. He sound like a man who know it's about to rain and he don't have no umbrella. I almost make my mind up not to watch.

But then I'm hearin book spines and pages flap and desks straighten. I hear bags bein zipped open and murmurs and silence, and I'm goin along with it and not once do I stop and equate these noises with the noises of students cooperatin. I let the background be the background around me, and before you know it behind me is thirty kids right on the same page of the book. I'm the only one who don't have Cassius's book cracked open.

Mr. Broderick go, Who would like to read, and more than five hands shoot up in the air.

There's somebody to read the part of Walter Lee and Beneatha and Lena and every time someone start readin, I peep the super-intendent sittin in the back to see if she's buyin it all. And Mr. Broderick, he moseyin along cuz he finally gettin the respect he feel he deserve. He have no idea of the miracle before his eyes. It's like, Ahem, he thinkin. This is the schoolin and the education I'm used to.

Jugglin two pieces a chalk in his hand, he go, Who thinks this dream of Walter Lee's will actually be successful?

Kimberly raise her hand and go, I think he gonna be successful because even though it's a liquor store, it's a business that could be all his, where he don't have to wake up in the mornin and answer to no one, and he know that and he determined.

Then Kowboy raise his hand.

I would like to agree with Kimberly and add on. I think some-times you want suttin so bad that nothin will stop you from gettin it, not even a dark hallway.

And Najee say, Yeah, I would like to agree with Kowboy, I mean Lashaun, and say my favorite character is Beneatha, cuz she poor, but she still wanna be a doctor, cuz it's good to have dreams and better to chase them.

And Ay Dawan say, What I wanna say to the conversation is I would like to see everybody in the book accomplish they goal, but they might not cuz I mean how many people in the ghetto do you see accomplishin they goals? It could be like that poem that said that they dreams might become dried-up raisins.

Mr. Broderick go, That was very astute of you, Ay Dawan.

And Ay Dawan smile all shy. It's hard to believe this was the same boy who did what he just did to the computer cart.

Maybe angels is in the air. Maybe God like playin around with his puppets when he bored. Maybe flingin us into predicaments is his way of entertainin hisself, all the while tellin us every wall we build can be crumbled down low. Maybe every hurdle that's set up before us is meant to be cleared. All I need is for the bell to ring, and the lady to go to her clipboard and renew all of us. And suddenly, that one-bedroom don't seem so bad. Now that it's lookin like I might keep both my jobs. Shoot, Imma ask my super-visor at the airport if maybe they have suttin part-time for Swan. I might could save up and get us back into the three-bedroom, and maybe run for the tenant board, cuz I know I could steer other people away from situations like these. Unlike the tenant ladies, I actually know how to talk to people.

But of course, if this fantasy I'm thinkin about is a cloud, here come the superintendent lady bustin thru it with her nose up, cuz this is what she get paid to do: sniff bullshit with her eyes closed.

And there she go rumblin up on the only student with her head down: Kandese.

Now, had it been straight survival mode, Ms. Chalmers woulda shook Kandese til she woke up. But Ms. Chalmers can't do that, and Mr. Broderick can only watch stunned.

It occur to me then that I'm the only one who know Kandese was not even spose to come to school today and am the only one who know where she slept last night and that it was by herself. She had her head down the last four periods, and I thought to myself, Poor child, go right on ahead.

The lady superintendent tap on Kandese shoulders. Kandese lift her head up a little and open one eye.

The lady go, I was wondering if you could tell me something about what you're reading.

Kandese go, I don't know.

The lady go, Excuse me.

I don't know nothin about this book.

Kandese put her head back down and the lady tap her again.

Don't touch me.

Surely, you can tell us something.

I said, Don't fuckin touch me.

You know how sometimes you think the room is quiet and then suttin happen and it go even deader—that's how it is now. And suttin about the way Kandese say it, the snarl in it, make the lady raise her hands like this and back away. But not before she bounce to Kowboy, Najee, and Ay Dawan's desks and flip thru they notebooks and find what she lookin for, which is that they don't have no notes. She make a whole cinema out of writin that down on her clipboard. Then she flag Ms. Chalmers and the AP, and they all step over the chocolate milk on they way out.

For a while, nobody utter nothin. We had it, and we lost it like *that*. The sadness sag round the room, and every now and then somebody will breathe in real quick like they tryna get the sadness out of they heart, too. It's so heavy everybody can barely keep they eyelids open. Nobody notice that Kowboy had stood up.

He take off the baseball cap he was wearin with the yellow brim and sticker still on it and hold it over his heart.

Guys, he say. I would like to apologize to all y'all. I would like to apologize to y'all for agreein with Kimberly cuz everybody knows her breath smell like green eggs and ham.

The class bust out laughin and Najee stand up and go, I also would like to apologize for sayin my favorite character is Beneatha. Honestly, I don't even know who the bitch is, it just sounded good.

And Kowboy turn to Ay Dawan and mock him in his squeaky voice, I would like to say suttin to the conversation . . . and by then some people is exaggeratin themselves out of they desks while Ay Dawan sit there with a dumb smile itchin on his face, and everybody in the room start actin like they can't see what's underneath theyselves.

I been savin up as long as I can. If you asked for a ledger right now, I'd say I have oh, about $1,294 pooled up in different envelopes around the apartment. The banks may have some of my money, but not all of it. With the first thousand I went right on down to the management office to petition for my old three-bedroom back, and you know what they had the nerve to say? That I gotta start from the bottom of the waitin list. Of course there was hot words thrown about, and I almost had to put my hands on the lady behind the computer, but they make it so that hands don't really do much now to further your cause. Plus they sit there and tell you stuff that make you totally hopeless anyway, like that the lady who live in your apartment now was on the waitin list since 1986.

Some people say I'm a good person, some people say I got my ways. I've never been one to deny any of that. I also believe that people who don't learn lessons should still get taught. If you with someone or a group of people for some time and you can't use the switch to turn off, and you end up bein insensitive, then that there is a problem. If you so-call work with kids and you have a day of things not goin your way and you can't separate that from not knowin what someone is goin thru and maybe givin them a break, well, *that there* is a problem too. Like for instance, if a superintendent or suttin come and you know you did bad cuz a girl had her head down and didn't do no work and now you worried you not gonna have a job next year or not save up enough money to travel barefoot to Kathmandu. You wouldn't go to that girl after and be like, Pick your head up off your desk right now, that's an order, just cuz you yourself feelin helpless. Then you don't decide to change your tone when, let's say, her boyfriend Najee, who in the class, too, raise his hand and go, Mister, give her a break. All you do is pitch your head away and wave him off til he forced to say, She in a shelter and her pops just died, and after all that you just kept sayin, So? So? and holdin on to this no-excuses business and the boyfriend is pleadin with you, Her daddy *died*, and you say, I . . . don't . . . care, real slow, with so much poison it's like you makin it known that you're talkin to every single soul in the class, includin the one other adult in the room. Then yes, I think *those* people should be taught suttin they will *never* forget. I can never be a bad person for thinkin that. Even if the girl who had her head down all of sudden get up with piston steam flowin out her nose, takes up the nearest object in her path, and brushes by me on the way to suttin wicked. And I don't stop her.

The Young Entrepreneurs of Miss Bristol's Front Porch

Y'all know how Bernita is. Making jokes about people so every-body still know she the Queen Bee. Everybody else get they jokes to they face, but she go behind Kandese back to clown her. Kandese say one of them New York phrases like *that's OD* or *it bees like that*, and Bernita wait to start makin fun of the way she talk, sayin she sound like a man, but not til we leavin the porch for the day.

Now look at her ringin Miss Bristol bell, crackin jokes before Kandese come out. Narely, she jus go along. She crackin up, snortin and shit, tryna get me to laugh, too, so Bernita don't get mad. Bernita say to Narely, That's funny, right? She punch her on her shoulder hard, and Narely automatically start laughin harder. Bernita lookin at me tryna to get me to laugh, tryna sound hoarse like Kandese. Her fat ass leanin on the porch railin, but she eyin me, remindin me she still the Queen Bee of Clinton. But she know I know her secret. She been makin fun of people to they face ever since we was all at the cafeteria at Ida B. Wells. Kandese the only girl who don't get the wrath. She also the only girl Bernita trade lip gloss with and say hey girl to.

Hehe, hehe, I go. She keep tryin harder, makin fun of Kandese, scrunchin up her face, talkin with her fingers like Kandese, but all

I see is Bernita's overweight self, her booty hangin over the top of her jeans. I get mad at myself for even givin her the laugh. And she know that too. She know she ain't foolin nobody.

The screen door pop open and, sure enough, here Kandese come out with all the candy, which she call merchandise. Bernita say, Hey, girl, and I shake my head at her. Kandese got all the stuff in a duffel bag. She unzip it like she done all summer. The Blow Pops is all in a small cardboard box that used to be for her grandmama's medicine. Same for the taffy, the Slim Jims and the hot cheese popcorn, all sellin for a quarter more than Old Man Duney sell dem for at the general store across the tracks. Kandese had glued some nice color paper around the box and wrote the prices in black marker all straight like she had dotted lines to help her. Narely, she stop her fake giggles right when the screen door opened, and now she grabbin the cartoon drawings and helpin Kandese hang them up. Bernita, she wait for a little bit to show us she can do whatever she want and then set up the combs and scrunchies, too.

Kandese do things smart and speedy. Like she got little signs that say sale on dem. She already know where she wanna put those. She thumb-tackin dem on the porch railin, flingin her hair every once in a while to get it out the way.

That weave get longer and longer every time I see you, Bernita say.

For a second I think she talkin to Narely cuz that sure sound like a suttin-starter.

Haha, you funny, Bernita, Kandese say the same way grown-ups say it when they pattin you on the head. But this ain't a weave. I told you I gets it straightened.

Then she twirl like the skinny models in dem magazines she be readin and I hold my smile. I wish I could snap back at Bernita fast like that, but every time she crack on my cornrows I jus freeze up.

Bernita look at me and Narely, finna see if we know she jus got sonned, and we pretend we still fixin up the candies on the porch. Then she put all her weight on her right foot and she ask, When we gettin our share of the money, anyway? We sold all this candy and we ain't seen near a dime, yet.

Then she look at me.

Be patient, girl, Kandese say to her. I told you I got stuff cookin. Mattafact—

She go into that duffel bag and pull out a tiny folded-up sheet with an address on it. The handwritin look jus like the one on the sale signs.

This is the address to the station that be playin the news, she say. Imma write to them and they gonna do a story on us.

I'm like, Yo, Kandese, that's a good idea.

My mama put on the news every night. I didn't know you could send them letters.

Ain't no news cameras comin down here, Bernita say. Cops don't even come here.

She love rainin on parades.

If we write the letter, they will, Kandese say. "Girls Start Business and Make Money." That headline is hot. Newspeople love when people start suttin new, and they the first to cover it.

Well, y'all go ahead and write y'all letters, Bernita say. Jus give me my share, and Imma buy me my stilettos.

Didn't I tell you Imma handle the money, Kandese say. I ain't gonna cheat nobody.

Bernita get quiet and everybody know who in charge again. The convo stop cuz some girls from down the block come thru askin for Blow Pops. Kandese say fitty cent. Narely cut on the radio. We officially open for business.

When Kandese first came at the beginnin of the summer, every Black girl on my block was waitin to get a look at her. Her grand-mama told us she hit a teacher with a ruler and got kicked out of her school in New York. I ain't even gonna front, I was sittin in the grass with the rest of the girls that sunny day when Miss Bristol's beat-up Oldsmobile pulled down our road. I wanted to see what she lookded like. I thought she finna be jus as fat as Bernita, seein how Miss Bristol say her teachers was afraid of her.

I damn nearly had to clean my eyes when I saw this lil-ass girl step out of Miss Bristol's car. Girl was like only three inches taller than me, and I'm not even thirteen yet. She was poutin by Miss Bristol's raggedy mailbox in her capris and sunglasses, and I jus kept thinkin, This is the eighth grader who told the teachers to go to hell?

When she got there, everybody was jus watchin her, waitin for her to say suttin evil. She lookded like she wanted to be anywhere but here. She had some notebook under her arm, and her thumbs on her cell phone busy typin a convo to somebody more important than us. So that's how those glamorous New York City girls are, I thought. I wish I had a cell phone, too, so I could call my girls and say things like, Girl, wear your heels tonight. We goin out to Times Square! But my mama would never let me have no phone. She don't even 'low me to use the cordless after a certain hour.

She ain't even look up once, I said to Narely.

Big Bernita butt in the way she do.

Bitch thinks she too good for Clinton, she said.

That was when she thought she could jus bully Kandese on some size shit.

But Bernita was right or at least that's what it lookded like for the first couple of weeks. Kandese was witnessin some class-A drama and actin like it wasn't no thang. Like when Toya mom bust out the house chasin a naked dude down the street. She was runnin faster than the devil with a slipper in her hand. The dude, who was twice her size, was tryna run with his pants in his hands. Everybody on the block who seen it was laughin. Later on, we found out that Toya mom had came back home thirty minutes after she left cuz she forgot her factory keys. She heard Jodeci comin out the one room she told Toya to always keep open. Everybody was screamin for Toya mom to catch the guy. It was like the Olympics. Except for Kandese. She seen the whole thing from beginnin to end sittin on her grandmama porch rockin back and forth.

Same thing when the tall bitch was chasin us, which is how this whole store business started. Everybody knew we stole from the general store across the tracks. It wasn't even a crime no more. We must had done it so many times. Bernita would go to the front counter and talk sex to Old Man Duney. Me and Narely jus dumped Cheetos, hot popcorns, Almond Joys, Slim Jims, and strawberry shortcakes in a sack.

But the last time we stole candy from Old Man Duney, none of us knew his grown-ass granddaughter was in the back room watchin. Narely slid a whole row of hot cheese popcorns in the sack, and the tall bitch came out the back with a hot comb. We was out.

Normally we put all the candy in the car on cinder blocks by Narely house, but when you bein chased and you runnin thru shrubs and hedges, you ain't got time to think. Narely seen the New York City girl on her porch and said, Hold this, and we was gone.

We couldn't come outside for a while cuz it turned out the tall bitch knew our mamas, Bernita found out and we had to walk with her to get our sack back. Nobody hold Bernita shit or she come stompin for you. I wanted to yell, Run inside, Kandese! But I was still into frontin like I was on Bernita side back then. I shoulda known Dese had spunk. She seen us and kept on rockin in her grandmama chair like nothin.

Where the candy at? Bernita asked.

Sold it, Kandese said.

I said where's the candy? Bernita repeated louder.

Only three candy bars left. All Almond Joys. Buy it next time, Kandese said.

Bernita grabbed the sack next to the rockin chair. Jus like Kandese said there were three Almond Joys. Me and Narely looked at each other, waitin for Bernita to blow up. We seen her snatch weaves, bite necks, stomp chicks out, all that. But she jus nodded and folded her arms. The dollar bills Kandese collected was layin there right next to the sack.

Miss Bristol got issues with her sugar. Now that Kandese been here, she help her out with reminders and things like that. Sometimes it seem like her grandmama forget why she got sent down in the first place, Kandese say. Her grandmama happy she got somebody to find the remote for her so she can watch her stories. She roll the cart for her grandmama when they at the market and her grandmama only stop when she see a member of her church group or someone she can share sweet potato pie secrets with. That sound like Miss Bristol all right, I think. Always tryna get a chore out somebody.

Today, I decide I ain't finna wait for Bernita and Narely slow asses. I walk up there by myself and help Kandese set up the candy. Miss Bristol's house is one of the oldest ones on our block. Some people say it been here since slavery days and I believe it. Yellow paint don't jus chip like that overnight. And it's the only house on this block that got a chimney. But this summer, it don't look old. It look like it got character.

It's one of dem really hot days and Kandese got a dirty fan stickin out of a window, but it's jus a slap in the face. Kandese say she miss New York, but she needed to get away even though it wasn't her choice. She talkin to me like I'm her therapist. I'm noddin my head up and down, but not too fast cuz she might jus realize what she doin confessin to a little girl. So I'm keepin it cool, lookin at her long hair, how she chew her gum all strong and confident. I'm thinkin about how many boyfriends she must got at home.

I had a hard year, she say, and I wanna ask, Why come you hit that teacher with a ruler? But instead I ask, Is you really gonna send a letter to them TV people?

She go, Yeah, but we both know Bernita ain't too fond of the idea, and I go, Bernita, Schmernita.

She laugh at me, run into the house, and come out with a piece of paper.

Read this, she say.

Dear WCMC,

Me and my friends got a business and we only thirteen and fourteen years old. We sell candy, combs, pitchers of famous people, CDs, scrunchies, and some fruits. We poor and everybody we know is poor, but we doin suttin positive for the community. I beleive you should videotape us and put us on TV cause we got $396 and we aimin for $500.

Sincerely,

Kandese Bristol-Wallace

P.S. We all respectful girls. Kind and got manners.

Wow, I guess that's how easy it is. You can jus send a letter and get put on TV. I never really thought about how the TV people find the news, but I woulda thought it'd be suttin more complicated than that. Like if somebody get shot, maybe a satellite from space send them a beep, beep. Then someone at the news station go, Looks like we got some news, and they jump in the van with the camera and that long microphone. But when Jamel got shot by the tracks two summers ago, I didn't see no vans. A lot of people was standin at his funeral cuz they wasn't enough chairs. I kept expectin the newspeople to show up but they never did.

This is a good letter, Kandese, I say.

She say, I made sure I wrote it in my best script to let them know—

Jus then Bernita come bubblin up the stairs with Narely and her own stretched-out forehead lookin like radiator rust. I freeze up, but Kandese is chillin. She hand Bernita the paper and say, Here's the first draft. Bernita read it, stay silent, and then scrunch up her face.

You spelled "believe" wrong, she say. She only know that cuz of the song Ms. Tingdale teach us.

Oh, Kandese say. She take her pen from her rockin chair and correct it. All better, she say.

Why you wastin your time writin letters anyway? Bernita ask. When the last time you seen teenagers on the news sellin candy?

She sound like a hater, but I know where she comin from. Every time we wrote letters in school, nothin happened. Ms. Tingdale say if y'all could have dinner with anybody famous who would it be? She say write about it. We smile and put our pencil erasers on our lips and go hmmm and write a whole paragraph. But we never get to have lunch with our person. She tell us come up with stuff to do that will make the neighborhood better. She say start the letter with "To Whom It May Concern," and we write it and we fold it up and put it in the envelope, but Whom never write us back.

This is different, though. Kandese got a real address and a real station. Plus we got almost four hundred suttin dollars and countin. Them newspeople would be silly if they don't put us on the TV.

Any other corrections? Kandese ask. Bernita go, humph. Kandese say, I'll take that as a no.

Bernita start tappin her toe. Well, I don't care about bout TV or none a that stuff. Jus gimme my share so I could get them stilettos I seen in the window. Sides, they wouldn't want my loud ass on the news anyway. Then she start laughin like it's the funniest joke in the world.

By loud ass, she mean, fat ass. She jab Narely, lookin for her to agree and to let her know she fat, too. Narely smile. It's a smile that say, Yes ma'am, but when Bernita ain't lookin, she smile another smile that say, I'm not as fat as her.

Jus need my stilettos, Bernita go.

Then she pretend she a model goin down a runway, but she stop as soon as she realize she got earthquake steps. That's when she go, Where that money, anyway? All playful. Is it here, is it there? She grab Kandese bag. Is it in this?

Kandese grab Bernita hand. My eyes want to jump out and pull Kandese hand away. Don't nobody do that to Bernita and live to tell the tale. Bernita keep laughin cuz that's the only thing she can do, but Kandese is holdin her and the porch ain't creakin no more. Kandese get high and humpy shoulders and the whole situation feel like thorns gonna start poppin out of dem. I'm lookin at Kandese up and down, tryna see if I can see the ruler girl in there. My armpits start ticklin, and I almost get scairt for Bernita. But Kandese shoulders go down again, and she let go. The porch start creakin again. She take the bag away from Bernita and pull out an envelope and a stamp. She lick the envelope and the stamp mad slow in front of her, walk down the stairs, half a block to the nearest mailbox.

Me and Narely stand waitin for what Bernita gonna say.

She walkin around like she finna give this county a makeover, Bernita say. Like she Mary Poppins and shit, bringin the hood joy.

Too many beats go by without nobody sayin nothin. Narely start laughin, huffin like an engine. Bernita happy again for the moment.

. . . .

Latoya come thru on Saturdays, see how her drawings sellin. Truth be told, nobody was touchin them papers with her little gods and goddesses on horses until Kandese started callin them classical art. Maya pay us to let her braid people's hair on the right side of the porch, and Toya be on the left biggin up her own work. On those days, we start early. We got a cardboard box of Airheads in dem. All the bags of chips we got is pinned up to the banisters. Miss Bristol don't care. She jus happy we around to snatch up to reach suttin for her. On these days, you see girls peek, chill, bargain over prices, talk shit, and leave with bags. By the time everybody gone, all that's left on the porch is hair and candy wrappers.

I don't know how Toya be showin her face so easy after her mom caught her bonin, but she do. When she get together with Bernita all they talk about is what channels they watch that they ain't posed to be watchin.

Toya stupid, though. Every cent she make off her drawings she turn around and give back to us with her Blow-Pop-fiendin self. She already bought five off the bat today. She leanin on the porch wit one a dem in her mouth and that's when Bernita come to her and say that's not how you posed to lick it. Bernita grab one of her unopened Blow Pops, take off the wrapper, push it slowly in the back of her throat and then pull it out. That's how you supposed to do it, she say. Latoya go, Na unh, na unh then she take her Blow Pop and slide her tongue around it and go, That's how. Narely watchin, pretendin to make sure the rest of the candy is in order.

Kandese ain't into talk like that, but it's Saturday. We make the most money on Saturday so she like whatever.

Let me get five more of those, Dese, Toya say, and Kandese ring it up.

Toya grab her pops. You can tell she got more ways to show Bernita how to lick them, and you can tell Bernita ain't worried about who buyin what, jus about outlickin Toya. It's hot and the sun's zappin our clothes off. It feel like every pit bull in every house on this street is barkin cuz they wanna get out the gate. It's a bad day for people with kinky hair.

Kandese go, Toya come back here. I'm thinkin finally she done had enough of people not workin. Toya and Bernita look at each other like, Yeah, maybe we did go overboard, and Toya walk over.

The money you jus gave me put us over $500, Kandese say.

Celebrate, say Toya. Celebrate, say Narely.

How? Bernita ask.

I know, Toya say, and then she leave.

Wow, $500, I think. That's probably how Oprah started. We could be like Oprah. We could be store owners. Not jus one store, a chain of stores. We could get so much money, we might not have to sell other people's candy. We could have our own brand of candy and sell our own products. We could have mansions and Kool-Aid finna be pourin out the faucets. I could have a big mink coat and step out limousines with big black heels that sound like the sound of fame.

My daydream go poof, and I see Toya walk up Miss Bristol steps with four boys. Or should I say men. They all at least sixteen or older and got scarves tied around they heads. One of them—the leader—got three scars on his face. Then Toya got the nerve to leave them there and disappear. My heartbeat go bump, bump, bump. I look over at Kandese. She already got a couple of cardboard boxes and ziplock bags with money in the duffel. She tryna zip up the whole thing fast but casual. I'm expectin her to say some little joke to make it all right, but she don't say nothin.

Congrajalashuns, the leader come up and say. I hear y'all got a successful business goin on round here.

Kandese look right past him. She holdin the duffel bag tight.

My bad, the leader say. My name is Wild One.

He put out his hand for her to shake it. His fingernails is long, and I can see the grime underneath them. For the first time this summer, it look like Kandese don't know what to do. She woulda left the dude hangin, but Bernita step right in and flutter her eyes at him. She got her back against the railin. Her titties is bustin out of her shirt, and there's spit out of the corners of her mouth, but she lickin it away. She shake his hand, and he go, This is a fine stablishmen, and the boys around him say, Fa sho, That's my word, and You ain't lie. Wild One look around and then go, Who responsible for all this? We all point to Kandese.

Wild One say, This you?

He say it so loud, cockin his head back to look at her real serious, his single braids bouncin a little on the side of his head. He point to his temple and say, Damn girl, you must be smart.

This is suttin. This is suttin. You smart, huh?

Kandese say, Iono.

Wild One say, You frontin, you know you is.

Kandese look at him like he the three-card monte guy, like she tryin not to let herself fall for the hustle.

Kandese say, Maybe.

Wild One say, Show me a report card or suttin.

Kandese say, Na.

C'mon, c'mon, Wild One say, and he look at his boys and they say, C'mon, c'mon.

Kandese look like she thinkin and finally go in the house real quick and come out with a piece a paper. Why she have it handy like that, I don't know. Anyhow, she offer it to Wild One like it's a piece of pie 'cept she still holdin on to it. Her thumb is over four of the grades. Wild One look at it with his face all concernt like he a parent, and he go, A 95 in eka, eka. He press his face closer to the paper and say, Ekanomnics, a 95 in ekanomnics. He put his hand up to give her a high five, but Kandese let his hand stay in the air a little before she give him a soft high five back. I wanna give her a high five, too, but I wonder which class was it when she went in on the teacher. How she get a good grade in that E class? She musta had a teacher like Ms. Tingdale.

Aight, Wild One say. We takin y'all to the lake to celebrate. His boys shake they heads. They all lookin at Kandese with that nasty-man look. They wanna all be her boyfriend at the same time, even if they gotta let me and my mosquito bites come along too.

This don't feel right. Kandese try to come up with an excuse to say no in a way that don't get the boys mad. Store closin, I gotta bring all the stuff back in the house, she say. But the boys say, Na, na, na, and it's 50/50 and Kandese could win, but Bernita step in.

Oooh, she say. Where you finna take us? Is y'all takin us on a date?

She push her chest so her titties is pokin out, and she pull up her pants jus so the rest of her could wiggle, too. Two of the boys look at each other and whisper suttin to theyselves. Now with Narely it's five on one, and I'm bout to cry cuz I ain't got enough guts to make it five on two.

Fine, Kandese say, liftin her duffel bag. Let me put this away.

Na, bring that wit you, Wild One say. He put his hand to his chin for a second. But there go Bernita again.

They might wanna buy some candy.

Wild One go, Yeah, that's it. We might wanna buy some candy.

Kandese pick up the bag slow, waitin for someone to change they mind.

At the lake, which is past the tracks by where the white people live, the water look like it's boilin. Wild One sittin in the grass next to Bernita. If there was a picture took of them, people would laugh at Wild One mad teeny tryna brush his knees on big-ass Bernita. They sittin in the grass pullin blades and throwin dem into the water. They giggling, and Bernita whisperin to Wild One, coverin his ear with her hand. She poke at Wild One zipper, and he go, Stop it, stop it, but he mean the exact opposite of what he sayin.

Kandese guy whisperin in her ear. He rubbin his beard on her, but every time he try to move forward, she shake her head. Maybe she worried bout the duffel bag, I think. She must get dudes by the swarms in New York City. So she should be handlin dem better than this. There's another dude with Narely. The only interestin thing about that is waitin to see when the dude gonna realize she not that interestin.

Why did Bernita get us into this situation? I think to myself. She always gotta drag people into her trouble. Don't nobody wanna be her real friend cuz of that. She violatin every rule Mister Rogers, Barney, and Officer Friendly ever taught anybody. Don't talk to strangers. Don't let people know you got money. Don't let people drag you to a place where nobody can hear you scream.

I wanna fast-forward to the end of this tape. Please God, tell me this turn out right. I'd be happy if in the end it show me in my bed with my 'jamas asleep like a feather. Please show how we got out this lake.

That's when Wild One pop his head up.

See how we help y'all celebrate in style, he say.

When nobody say nothin, he say it louder, expecting yeses. We nod our heads.

And y'all the billionaires here, he say. Y'all should be takin us to the movies or the mall or suttin.

And Bernita jump up at the wrong time as usual.

I would take y'all out, she say. But we ain't even get our share of the money yet.

He turn his eyes on Kandese like the mother in the movie do when she find out the little white girl done told a lie.

This true? he ask, ready to take back that high five he gave her at the porch.

We savin it, Kandese say, and I can tell she annoyed that she even had to say that much.

But it's they money, too. They worked for it, he say.

Wild One, the talk-show host. His boys, the audience with they mm-hmms. Bernita got her chin up at the sky like she tellin herself this is a nice sky, but she really jus happy somebody else talkin for her. Kandese don't say nothin, not cuz she disagree though. She never disagreed with Bernita in the first place. I wanna step in and be like everybody is supposed get they money, duh, but she tryna do suttin more important, stupidhead. But I can't cuz I'm jus a watcher. That's what's wrong with me.

Kandese sit there silent. That's all she can do. When you tryin to do suttin great, you can't explain it to someone who's too caught up in the everyday to understand.

Let her get her share, Wild One say.

One of the other dudes speak up. Let her get her share, ma.

Then another one whisper, Look at her poutin. Bet she'd put that booty on you, make you work. But he whisper it loud enough for her to hear.

I gotta go, Kandese say. She let the boys know why by the way she stand up. That make Wild One stand up, too, veins runnin up his arm. They both at eye level, his eyes more redder.

Let her get her share, he say. This time it don't sound like him. It sound like the wolf he got inside him that he tryin not to let out. Before he say this, I was pretty sure everybody here knew boys was not posed to hit girls. Now I ain't so sure.

It look like Kandese ain't so sure either. Plus, there's suttin thick that's burnin the sides of everybody face, and we lettin it burn Kandese face the most. The longer Wild One stand with dem bulldog nostrils, the thicker that suttin get and back Kandese into a corner. She jus go ahead and stop the fight. She unzip the duffel, count ten ten-dollar bills out slow enough for anybody to change they mind if they wanted to. She don't know that while she countin, he countin, too, peekin in the duffel and seein the type of money he prolly never seen all in one place. So what the wolf do? He come up with another idea.

Let Bernita hold on to the cashbox, he say. Kandese jus lookin at him like is this the weed talkin. Either way, he serious, and this close away from woof-woofin. I don't think even Bernita wanted to take it that far, but right now she a watcher too. Watchin Kandese hold on to the duffel bag and her dreams.

And just like that, Wild One, he take a step forward. He take the bag away from her. As if Kandese wanted to give it to him in the first place, and he jus helpin her out. Now, Kandese hands go from holdin suttin to holdin nothin. Everybody around her go from being silent to being silenter. But what's sad in this whole thing is Wild One ain't the criminal here. No, no, no. He jus a dude who did suttin. The criminals is us people around him, the people watchin someone shake someone else awake from a dream and not doin nothin to stop it. It make me feel so bad, but the thought in my head—and I know it's in other people's heads—is, Kandese, please don't say nothin else.

But she do.

We was gonna show the TV people that money, she say.

And what she say float out to the lake with the air and the blades of grass we done pulled the whole afternoon. If that letter was a bird, we done already threw rocks at it until it died. Kandese turn around and walk away. Then the dudes look at me and Narely like, I think y'all need to walk away, too.

I see Miss Bristol's Oldsmobile when she and Kandese gettin ready to go to the bus station. God, August always sneak up on you from behind. I jus think bout how all us girls was curious to see her when she first came thru for the summer. Now, I doubt none a them would even yawn if they found out it was her last day here.

I see it all out my window bars. People is funny and borin when they don't know people is watchin them. Kandese suitcase is messin up the grass cuz she had to drag it. Then again, everything else done messed up Miss Bristol grass, french fry containers and flyin newspapers. There's that broken door on the Oldsmobile that everybody know about cuz they hear Miss Bristol tryna shut it before the cock crow every mornin. There she is now tryna open the door to let Kandese get in. She gotta lift it up and push it in at the same time. She do it like five times, but the door make the same sound when you coughin out mucus and jus pop back out. Then Kandese try it, but nothin doin. All that jus make her more crouched down and sweaty.

I wonder if she think she a loser in her head. True, it was hard to sell candy after that whole Wild One shit, but most girls wouldn't a bounced back like that. But I still wonder. I wonder if she feel like she maybe gettin kicked out. She cursin anybody in her head? Is it Wild One? Is it Bernita? I wonder if she thinkin bout that bitch, how she didn't show her face that last month. She could have at least tell us what she done with the money. Give us that.

I wanna run up and say, Don't think you a loser, Kandese. Bernita got hers. And while you was inside those last days, gossip was flyin back to us. Gossip about Bernita and her belly. How her mother caught her undressin and saw it and chased her with a cast-iron skillet, screamin, You ain't bringin illegitimates in this house. How she called Wild One on the phone, and he said, It could have been a whole train of people if you know what I mean.

Miss Bristol and Kandese finally get that car door to shut. All Kandese stuff in the back seat, so the Oldsmobile ride slower and lower than it supposed to. I know once it ride past me, that's it. The candy, the money, the business all done. My godmother cleans the floors in the hospital, and when I pull the blind up, I see her walkin up the street. She always lookin behind her back, speedin up, to get away from the outdoors. Like every doorstep gonna swallow her up. Like roots finna spring up from the concrete, grab her ankles, and hold her there forever. Even in the spring when the animals started talkin again, everybody racin to get to they landin. Everybody else's landin was jus poison. That's why it was weird to see Kandese hangin out on Miss Bristol's porch like that because until then porches was like quicksand. The longer you was out on them, the more people saw you dyin. But she made it different. Everybody wasn't jus goin from work home, or summer school home. They was chillin at our store. Even if they wasn't buy nothin, they stopped by, checked us out. Bought some fruit, got their hair did. Said, Hey, y'all. Kandese store made it like that.

Now it's over, and I watch the Oldsmobile go slow down the street, beggin for somebody to pull it over.

Now that Kandese gone, I'm the one back to helpin Miss Bristol. I gotta tighten the plastic on the couches and make sure her medicine is in that box that tell what day a the week to take it. Every time the phone ring, my heart jump. I want it to be Kandese. Every time I get done with a chore, I wanna take that photo album Miss Bristol got under the coffee table and see if Kandese or her mother got a picture in it or suttin. When Miss Bristol barge in, I hope she catch me and say she got more. But all she ever got for me is a fake smile and more stuff to do. Every week, I go to Miss Bristol's and do her chores. If I don't do dem all the right way, she hold her heart all dramatic and say to me, I could die any day now.

The Saturday before school start, I wait in the front room til it's reasonable enough for me to say, Miss Bristol, I gotta go for the afternoon. When I do, she say, Wait. So there I am with my new school backpack, tryin not to sit my butt down too heavy on her couch so she don't tell my mama I'm disrespectful. I'm glad school startin, and I can get out of this smelly-foot house. I made sure I cleaned up extra good so she won't come flaggin me back in the streets. Now I jus need the word and, deuces, I'm out.

Thirty minutes pass by and I'm like, oh hell na. So I go look for her. She in the kitchen and she obviously done forgot about me. When she finally notice me, her shoulders rumble and then stop when she see I wasn't no burglar. There's a pile of mail on her sticky table. She shuffle through it, find one. When she open it up and read it, her face go blank. After a while, she give up and hand me the envelope. I hope it's money, but then I realize I ain't seen Miss Bristol give nobody a dime in all my years of knowin her. Prolly a note for my mama.

I look at it, and it don't even got me or my mama's name on it. Mattafact, it got Kandese's name. The address look mad official. It say suttin, suttin, suttin, television studios. Oh shit.

I wanna use tiger teeth to open it up, but instead I slide my finger thru it jus like grown-ups do when it's jus another bill they gotta pay. Then I see the folded letter, and I hold it like I shoulda washed my hands. But by now I know what it gonna say. I know it gonna say suttin like thank for your letter, we will consider your words very carefully, and continue to tune in. I already know I'm gonna read it nine hundred and ninety-nine times and that each time I read it is gonna make me sadder. By the time I get to a thousand, I'm jus gonna say, along with everybody else, that it's jus one of them letters they send to everybody. By the five thousandth time Imma ask why come Kandese hit the teacher with that ruler, and the answer ain't gonna surprise me. Then Imma ask why come the news cameras ain't here yet and laugh. And by the last time I read it, I ain't even finna be askin questions like that no more because Imma have the answers for all dem questions myself, and dem answers is gonna make me feel safe. Safe in my bubble with the rest of the Bernitas.

Camaraderie

was at the Secret Lounge on Twenty-Third Street swirlin the straw in my drink. I looked up and seent this foine light-skinned brother. He had an eight-pack that I could lay down and type on. He was the type of nigga you'd let do whatever.

I said to the bartender, Whip him up a Cosmos.

The bartender said, He look like he havin fun, right?

The dude seent who the drink was from. Before I could say, I'd like to know you better, he turned away with my drink in his hand, took off his shirt, and started humpin his pelvis at this other dude. I wanted to cry.

Outside the club, everybody was done and tryna fish. Qua and his twin, Quen, was doin pull-ups on the traffic pole. Qua hopped down when he seent me.

He said, Boo, all this bottom lip stuff need to stop. You been like this two weeks.

I didn't know it then, but when I look back at how everything went wrong, it go back to that night.

Forget what I did to Katrez.

Wait, you ain't seen the video? Crazy fan and Katrez? I was

about to say. I can't go nowhere without someone tappin me on the shoulder, sayin, You that guy?

But I'm not some lunatic, thank you very much. It's not like I murdered her. The bitch is still alive. The internet make it look like I need a restrainin order. They make it look like I'm an angry person. I'm the biggest Katrez fan on this earth. She the only singer that move me. Not Beyoncé. Not Rihanna. Now all this drama done put a pause on everything. All my hair dreams.

See, that night after the club, we went back to my apartment. My head was down mopin. Qua was shovin me on the arm to snap out of it. He had his eye on the fluff that was comin out the couch that outlived my uncle and aunty. He was lookin at all the pictures of Katrez I had up on the wall. He was like, Wow, you really are a fiend. Quen was there, too, not talkin.

Dary, Qua said, pullin my arm. You can't keep gettin like this every time a man turn you down.

It's not even about that so mind your business, I said.

Then what is it about? he asked me.

I showed him the note they taped to my door. The one that said I got sixty days to move out. I told him the old ladies on the tenant committee was tryna fight it. But even if they get me more time, I still wouldn't have money for no rent.

Oh, he said.

Then he flipped the paper over twice like he was stumped.

It's jus a problem with funds, he said. Dary, I told you this over and over. You gotta market yourself. There's so many people who wanna meet you and get to know you more.

Qua, not tonight, please.

What would Katrez do? She'd be about her business. You do that homework I told you to do?

He was talkin bout how I was supposed to make a list of my talents and they was gonna interview me about it.

Yeah, I said.

Quen, press record on your phone. And?

Ain't too many things I'm good at.

Go on.

Doing hair, listenin, and good in bed.

I pulled my aunty's old blanket over my head. Qua smirk like what I said went along with his plan.

Stop recordin, Quen. There go your brand right there. Rich men who need someone to talk to.

What I say about that, Qua?

To understand all of this, you must know about Qua. What can I say? He out there. Remember Sisqó? Sisqó with the yellow hair? Thong, tha-thong, thong, thong? Qua did his with yellow drink powder. It looked good. I told him, too. Said you look good. Until that night it rained, and he was at the restaurant drippin juice on the bar.

Qua'll fuck you in those beat-up rooms in Chinatown. He'll see you on the train, and suck you in with his eyes. He'll let you put it in that same night. We was in the parkin lot one time. This dude he was talkin to said I'm poz. Qua said, That's fine, just pull out. That's what he said. And waited like two months before he got tested.

It had to be like last year April Qua brung his first Prada bag around. I said, Where did you get that? He said, What's that supposed to mean? I said, It's supposed to mean you have no job.

From my boyfriends.

I looked at him like yeah, aight, okay.

You wanna know what I do? Fine.

He pulled his iPad. Soon, it was made clear. A video of him on all fours gettin done by a white guy. In the video, he was yellin, Mercy, mercy.

And I'm getting paid. And so could you.

Whatever, Qua. You puttin diamond bits in your sunglasses and buyin scarfs. You getting paid da da da. You do you. Why you so thirsty to put me on? You don't share nothin. Not no money, not no dick, not no ideas. The more he was goin around sayin, It don't feel like work, the more I was like, Wouldn't be me.

Besides, my aunty who's in her grave said, Too much love will kill you. She said that cuz of what my mother was doin. How I woke up in the mornin one time and she was in the livin room on her knees with a stranger. And how I showed the kids in my class what she was doin, and how ACS snatched me outta that house so quick I don't remember the phone number. I agree with aunty 100 percent, even though had that not happened I wouldn't have moved in with her and Uncle Holcombe. And if I didn't move in with her and Uncle Holcombe, I wouldn't have seen the dolls in the closet that she sold at the church. And if I hadn't seen those dolls, I wouldn't have discovered stylin their hair.

I told Qua I'm a businessman, not a stylist, and definititely not somebody on the prowl to kiss all the men in the world.

Look at all the movies. Anytime they show us, we gotta be on our knees. It can't jus be us regular. If they did a movie about my buildin, they wouldn't care about the two dudes upstairs who been together for years. They wouldn't show when they jumped the broom in the bingo room. How everybody was happy even though it wasn't official. They wouldn't show the butch lady in 4D who is always wearing a necktie and got a computer certificate. They don't care about that. That's why we gotta be more. But some people is hell-bent on makin you a prostitute.

I'm not tryna make you a prostitute.

This us on my same couch with his brother after that night at the club.

Look, here's you and here's your friend. Qua said, scoopin out two teddy bears from a toy chest I had when I was a boy.

He there for company, for camaraderie. He want an evenin with you. You askin him questions. What's your deepest thoughts? What you dream bout? You ever look at the stars? That's all it is, really. Stop messin around with these dolls and go make some-body feel good.

But like I said to Qua all they think we do is run around givin each other sex. They think you gay was cuz suttin happened, even though you tell them you knew since the very first time you was at the public pool and you seen the lifeguard's penis accidentally come out his shorts like a beaver. Again, that's why I be careful what I do. I do what I do behind closed doors. I don't be publicizin or braggin. When I'm around straight men, I make them feel comfortable. Even if I gotta change how I talk. That make it easier for all us. That's what I tried to tell Qua. Plus, my aunt when she was alive said you can sell whatever you want, but it's over when you start sellin you.

But see this is what had happened.

Mimi who live two floors up, she used to let me come over and help out with her customers. When it come to hair, everybody know this her buildin. I was shampooin her clients' hair, drapin them. She was payin me $20 a session. Between that and what my aunty left me, I was doin aight. Then one day she gonna turn around and say, I don't need you no more. That same day the covers to one of the outlets in my place came off. All you seen was sparks. Then my heat got turnt off. Then trash started comin out my shower. Before you knew it, what my aunty left me ran out. My credit cards was maxed out. I couldn't sleep.

I'd be at the library workin on my résumé and they'd just blow up my phone. *This is your third notice.* I wanted to be like, Bitch, I've noticed everything. I just don't have the money.

I applied for several hairstylist positions. They didn't want me. Applied to *Essence*, got the dial tone. And I still had to get my rent money. I still had just sixty days. Then, I started thinkin.

Is it really an issue if you talkin to them first? Isn't that like a regular date? Couldn't you have it in your mind to do it for free, and if they gave you money, that would be on them? Isn't makin a connection different from just gettin nekkid?

I also thought: It's practice servin clients.

See when I start Snip Hip, it's not just gonna be about hair. It's gonna be a whole experience. Mimi got it wrong. She into that wham, bam, thank you, ma'am. You go to her in 14D for some extensions, she gonna have you out of there in thirty minutes. But with Snip Hip, you not just getting your hair did. You gettin your soul did. You gettin someone that's gonna listen to you.

Ever since I was born, I knew I was gonna be great. I have the whole package, a carin personality, talent, photo friendly. I have many avenues. Before hair, I could have done makeup. When we was at Sephora, me and Teddyloo used to pull customers to the side for consultations until the hatin ass manager put a stop to it. I always have ideas in my head.

You know how many people out there not workin for a dream? They sweepin, carryin boxes? Not me. You gotta be ready for your big break. You got to grow. You got to block out all the chirpin.

The more I thought about it, the more I said maybe Qua was right. Maybe I should be more concernt about my brand.

Not too long after that consideration, I ran into Mimi at the beauty store on 125th tryna apologize and soak me in pity talkin bout, I was goin thru some things with my rent, but I'm somewhat good now blase-bla and I could throw you a couple of dollars this month to wash some of my clients' hair.

I told her no need, I had this therapist business I was workin on.

Therapist, like psychology and stuff? she asked.

Yup, and my friend Qua know mad clients who need me.

Oh.

And that made me feel all right. Even though the senorita at the counter wouldn't let me see the blow-dryers and I almost had to crack her display case.

Like I said, these is upscale men, Qua said all giddy. They the boss of they company. They fathers. They uncles.

This time we was in their brownstone, the one they grandma left them that last time I checked online was worth a million dollars. That is, if they fix it up and stop livin in complete darkness.

I didn't tell him yes—not all the way. I had only hit him with, If I were to do this. Still, it was nerve-rackin cuz he was talkin like it was the first day and I was goin thru trainin.

They give you fake names, Qua said, but I be stealin they wallet and googlin them, he said. Lawyers, presidents of companies. I had this one dude who wanted me to feed him dog food. I was supposed to put a leash on him, lead him butt naked to the bowl. This other dude made me shit in the tub. After he kept dippin his toe in it and sayin, Man, that's warm. I'm tellin you, Dary. It's easy. They jus want the gushy. But for you that's not the main thing. For you, you talkin to them. You listenin to them cuz they wife don't. Ain't that right, Quen?

Quen broke his neck noddin. He was sittin on the floor barefooted, tryna eat the Chinese food with the chopsticks.

I was givin Qua a hard time, makin fun of his whole show. I was thinkin: I might not even have to take my clothes off. I was thinkin: maybe I'm the type they pay $5,000 jus for the conversation.

Dary Dadilly, Qua kept on. Fun and late-night camaraderie.

That's not my last name, I said.

You not supposed to use your real last name. This is your brand. See how easy that run off the tongue? Any time someone ask, What the deal, they gonna think of, what the dilly, and they gonna know Dary the dealy.

It's one of those things you do it once and then you gonna feel comfortable doin it, he said. It don't gotta be forever. And guess what, I got someone for you. I already texted him, too. I told him you're eight inches tall. Booked you up for the Ritz in DC next weekend.

Here's the thing, he said. I found out Katrez is gonna be there that same date signin autographs.

The Katrez. She had my heart ever since I heard that one song "Rude Boy." The one that go, You changed my world, you make me fiend for it, fiend for it. I heard that and the next thing you know I was in the apartment, cleanin, with the whole album in the background.

Me and her got the same soul. She glamorous and I'm glamorous. She got the boy-girl thing down and I got the boy-girl thing down, too. She a mogul that got her own handbag line and I got Snip Hip. If I could meet Katrez in person it would be a fantastic dream come true. That was all I was thinkin.

But all it take is your friend settin up an appointment for you, and your life could change forever for the worse.

Qua and Quen had took me down to the Port Authority for the Greyhound. They blew kisses at me. The bus smellt like old popcorn. I thought that was bad until I had to booboo and smellt the toilet.

It kept echoin in my head: You really goin thru with this. I tried to block everything out. People wanted to be nosy. I banged my fist on the window, and everybody turnt around. I said, Listen up, if anybody in here got an eye problem, let me know. That was the end of that. I took a nap and then woke up in the nation's capital where Martin did his speech at. I seen the snipers on the government buildings that will shoot you. The Iraqistani dude in front of the station acted like he ain't even want let me in the cab, but then he sucked his teeth and took me to the Ritz.

The room had not one piece of lint on it. The bathroom had all these nice soaps and white robes hangin off a hook. The fridge had all the Sprites you could ever drink in your life. I stole a soap and put one of the robes on. I slank my ass down on the bed. It felt like I was backstrokin in the ocean. I thought about Katrez.

Yeah, sister, I usually get the Waldorf.

But then the voices came. They said Dary you here to fuck and get money. You a disgrace. You never wyled out with dick before. You got a type. Samuel Jackson, Lenny Kravitz, and Rick Fox. Dary, once you do this ain't no comin back.

I was all fucked up so I called Qua.

It's nice, right?

I don't know, Qua.

What you mean you don't know?

I ain't wanna do this.

Don't do it, he said. You don't have to.

Whew, I said.

My only concern is what you gonna do about that rent you owe. And that hotel room I booked back when you first said yes. Imma need that investment back. Just let me know when I can have all that money.

There was nothin I could say.

Dary, we friends. You gotta see there's more to the world than Banneker Terrace. You gotta see what you missin.

I hung up feelin in jail. I was mad scared. I figured, Dary, you need to calm down, so I went on my phone. Then I went to sleep on the king size. But not for long cuz there was a knock on the door.

His suit was plaid and baggy. His shirt was blue. His tie was brown. He was carryin a briefcase. Qua was right. They a type.

He bent down on one foot to pull his shoe off. His scalp was blam in my face. It had leopard spots. I felt sorry for him.

He said, You're Quanell's friend?

I said yes.

He put his shoes down at the foot of the bed.

I wondered should we talk, but he was lookin down every time I wanted to say suttin. I felt feelings wellin up, so I went to the bathroom and sobbed in the mirror. I had to get myself together. He was out there waitin. I dabbed my tears and went back. The nigga was sittin on the bed lookin sorry. I swear that's the only thing that made me scootch over and kiss his mustache. He kissed my eyebrows.

My heart was like badoom, badoom. I went lower and pecked him on the neck. He took off his glasses and put them on the table next to the bed. Everything was feelin nice and okay. Then, he palmed my head down to his penis, which he took out the zipper.

All of a sudden my mouth started workin. He was mad aggressive. I wanted to stop right there. I wanted to be like, Oh please.

Afterward, the sheets was glazed with sweat and semen. With him like he was and me like I was, I knew there wasn't gonna be no type of camaraderie. I tried anyway. I scootched my ass next to him on the bed. I said, So the first thing I would like to know is— he fell asleep.

I stared at the ceilin. I thought, Dary, you a prostitute. Everything you ever wanted to do in life was a failure. You ain't shit, Darius, and I went to sleep.

He was still knocked out when I woke up. I seen he had put money on my side by the lamp. The bills was glistenin. It was enough to cover my rent for a whole month and then some. They was shoutin take us, stupid. But I left them right there.

My thought process was: if I didn't take it, I ain't do nothin wrong.

I said to myself, Dary, you a positive person. You don't need this. Put your chin up. Sit up. Go get your dream. Stop feelin sorry for yourself. So I got up and took my ass to Best Buy.

The only time I ever seen Katrez in person was in New York four years ago. Me and Teddyloo had both called in sick and went down to see her at Madison Square Garden. That's when she came out with the second album, the one with the video in the candy factory and they had her come down the stage in a hot air balloon. She had this two-piece pink workout outfit with kneepads and gold jewelry. Her hair was wet. You could tell she was cold, but it was still cute. She put her hand out to the crowd. A bunch of us in the fourth row reached for her. I touched her fingers. I screamed, I love you, Katrez. She didn't hear me. I thought they was gonna replay it on the Jumbotron, but they didn't.

Ask me what I remember bout the second time at Best Buy. Not a thing.

Don't remember the sign at the bottom of the escalator. Don't remember the thousand suttin people. I couldn't tell you how Katrez even got in the store. Did she walk past us? Past me? What was her outfit? You could say girlfriend had on the black corset with all the bandannas of the rainbow. I'd be like, Okay—and?

I don't even know how I got from two hundred suttin in line to one hundred suttin, to fiftieth to third. I do, but it's all blurry. All I remember is Katrez's brown skin gleamin in front of me. How she put out her fingers for me and her nails was did up with rhinestones in them. How limp and delicate they felt, but good. After that, I got my version. Katrez got her own.

I only heard her side of it once. It was on the late show.

She told them she was signin autographs in DC, and it was my turn. I had the *Astronaut Me* CD, so she knew I was a real fan. I said, Hey there, and she signed my CD. She told me, Thank you and keep listening.

According to her, I walked away, but changed my mind, came back, and said, You know I do hair, right. She said, Fabulous.

Yeah, let me show you.

Okay.

In her version, I mimed with her hair what I would do. Like huge box braids and here's your punk piker look and your updo.

Here's you in the next *Coming Front* video—fierce. She was humorin me til she seent the girl behind me and said, The girl behind you has been real patient. I don't wanna keep her waitin.

The next thing is a lie cuz she claims I still kept my hands on her hair. That I said and she quote, I was thinkin you could take me on the road. I could be your personal stylist da da da. We'd be like best friends.

She swore I definitely heard her, but just in case she said, Get off my hair now, please.

This is where she's convinced that I, all of a sudden, had her hair gripped. That she was swervin tryna get loose. That I was sayin, I'm sorry, I'm sorry, we got off on the wrong foot. That I was beggin, Please, Katrez, stay after this autograph session. Let me do your hair just once. I remember havin my hands on her hair, but why would I beg?

Finally, she said she was screamin, and that Tony who's always on the road with her had to come up and taze me.

How did you feel? the host asked her.

I felt bad for him, she said. I already have a stylist who I really love.

You don't think I realize everybody's goin da da da about me? That these tenants here is runnin around talkin about what I did to Katrez?

I said it a million times. The only thing that hurt me was the video cuz I know how people's minds work.

Besides that, I don't care. I don't care I had to face the judge. I don't care about the six months. I don't care what they said about me on TMZ. I said that to the bitch at the clinic who recognized me when she was drawin blood.

I know you prolly like, Well, Dary, if you Mr. Eff the World, why won't you come out your apartment? You embarrassed? You satisfied with Ho Hos out the vendin machine? You gonna let the tabloids ruin your life? This is ridiculous. It's been months.

You might possibly have a point. Or did you consider that maybe while everybody is sniffin up my butt crack, I might be makin moves? That maybe what you think is me lockin myself in here is me weighin my options? That maybe I could have suttin spectacular lined up? That maybe the magic crystal was right here with me all along? Well, guess what? It was. Suttin for my brand stuck the other day. The best idea I ever came up with. It's marvelous. It's gorgeous. It's all the above. You wanna know what it is, don't you?

lite feet

dear ms. singleton,

u no me already, but in case u 4got my name is najee. i'm 12 years old and i'm ritin this to tell u & everybody that i'm kwittin lite feet. neva thot i wud say this but i wish there wuz never no such thing as lite feet and i wish i never joind it. my life is a mess now. my own mother is scard of me. does anybody wanna read this? i dout it. imma tear this paper up when i'm threw.

i luvd lite feet in the begning. lite feet is dancin in the trains like the kids u see. well its not just dancin in the trains its dancin piriod. everybody be in a cirkul takin turns gettin lite on they feet doin the aunt jackie doin the chicken noodle soop anything wile people clap. that's how i had met mookie and kowboy.

we wuz turnin it up in mr. borderick class every1 wuz bouncin off the walls showin him no respeck. the para ms. dallas wuz tryin to shut us up but she wuznt tryin hard cuz no one like mr. borderick cuz he always sayin he went to harvid. sum1 had a boom box and put it on and things got live.

somebody get lite, somebody yelld.

kowboy jumpd in. he had a bandanna and he wore it like a blindfold and he wuz stompin the voise on the beat sed, ur a jerk, ur a jerk.

i jumpd in and the class wuz into it but not really into it cuz i'm fat so its hard to stay with the timpo. im better at tellin jokes that make every1 crack up.

but mookie jumpd in and the class explodid. he had 1 of his feet in his hand and jumpd over it with the other 1. he climbd on the desk and did a backflip off it. the class wuz like ah ah. the girls wuz wipin us down. mr. borderick wuz havin a fit.

he sed thats enuff thats enuff. im sick of dis!
we kep dancin.
the principle came in and the class got dum kwiet.
whos the main kulprits the principle sed.
mr broderick sed those 3.
the principle sed u guys again and eskortd us out and we blew kisses at every1.

that wuz dum wild, i sed when the deans wuz in the offis thinkin about suspindin us.
we shud start a group or suttin, kowboy sed.
i'm down, mookie sed.
cool, we all sed.

i don't know y i get in so much trouble at skool. i try to mind my business but the teachers r always settin me up. kimberly b talkin and they b sayin kimberly quiet down and they b smilin when they say it cuz kimberly gets good grads but hav it be me and theyll b like najee get the hell out of my classroom, thats why u'll never b nething. i like skool a lot. i just can't read good and rite good. the words get jumbld in my head and b4 you know it i hav a huge head ake. mr. borderick says i shudnt rite my composishuns like i'm textin on the fone and he says i shud stop bein illitrate and read at home for plaisur. i do that sumtimes. i read cheats for call of duty and 2k basketball stats, but i don't get any better. we'll b in mr. borderick class readin of mice and men and i won't know what the heck is goin on so i'll turn to kowboy and be like kowboy ya mama face look like a squashd acorn and he'll laff and be like ur breath smell like jesuses sandals and i'll laff too hard and mr. borderick wud dial the classroom fone and be like hello mr. cameron mr. cameron i need asistanse.

kowboy is always doin stuff like that. we call him kowboy cuz hes only 13 and got a full beard and sidebirns. if u eatin bacon egg and cheese he'll come rite behind u and snatch it and eat it and go hmmm that wuz delicious. he always doin stuff like that and peepul say kowboy ur crazy and they laff but when i do it every1 says najee y u tryna be like kowboy be ur own man.

to tell the trooth i don't know y mookie hung wit us. he wuz not one of the goodies, but he wuz not one of us bad kids neether. he wuz into dancin and he new we new he wuz the best. im not just sayin that cuz of what happend.

at our skool's kultural show we korograffed a performens. kowboy and me put our hands out and mookie pretent it wuz a turnstile and hoppd it and got lite. he took his braids out on purpose the day b4 and let it out on stage. all the gurls wuz sweatin. the audeens stood up the hole time and mr. nyim sed u guys shud be doin this instead of causin mischif.

it wuz kowboys idea of us hittin the train. he sed he wuz tired of his $ bein yung and he knew a frend who made a lot of bread. but nun of us knew how to go abot it. so we sed lets start wit the 2 train cuz thats closses to banneker terrace. i been livin in banneker terrace since i came out the womb. people say its scary cuz its in the news all the time. this person got shot this person got stabbd, but it dont make a diffrinse to me.

anyways i had told my mom i wuz goin out 2 play in the court-yard when i wuz really goin out wit kowboy and mookie. kowboy brung his stirioo. i wor my air force 1s the 1s i dont wer noweer not even 2 play ball.

dont act like a pair of bitches, kowboy sed when we wuz goin to the 125th stop.
i'm here, mookie sed.
i gulpd cuz i knew people wuz gonna stare at us.
its just dancin, mookie sed.
what if were whack, i aksd.
then we go to the next train stoopid, mookie sed.
on the 2 train me mookie and kowboy stood by the poles. it wuz crowded. nobody sed nothin.
kowboy wuz pickin his teeth with his long dirty fingernail and he pushd me in front and sed say somethin, najee.

everybody do you mind if we do a show, i sed to the train.

they can't hear u, kowboy sed.

he took the stirio out my hands and sed, i gotta do everything myself.

everybody we gonna get lite for u.

this pretty lady with shoppin bags lookd at us for 1 second and then lookd down at her receets and dis other guy put his head back in his newspaper. kowboy flickd the music on u cud feel the base in the floor. i tried to dance and flip my hat in the air but it fell on the floor. mookie is double jontd so when it wuz his turn he did dis thing where he foldd his elbows inside out. that cot some peepuls attention breefly. when kowboy turnt off the stirio nobody clapped.

wed appreshate a donashun, kowboy sed walkin up the ile with a black bag he got from imrans bodega.

he went to the guy wit the newspaper and sed, donashun.

the guy wit the newspaper sed, no.

i wantd to cry when he sed that.

kowboy sed, fuck this.

mookie sed, fuck this.

i sed, fuck this.

we dint hit no trains for weeks.

meanwile things wuznt goin so good in skool. mr. borderick gave us this progris report and it sed i read and rite worser than a 1st grader.

they sed to come to tootorin durin lunch and i agreed but i wuz in the lunch room and ay dawan sed carmelo is better than lebron and by the time i got done flamin him for his stoopidity the bell rang and i got in trouble for skippin. mr. borderick is always sayin najee, you hav no interest in ur own education but i dont say, but i do, mr. borderick cuz he wudnt believe me. but someday im gonna get better at readin and ritin words and i'm gonna read all the same books mr. borderick read at harvid and we'll be two smart people havin a conversashun. but sojourner truth m.s. 151 be bringin me down. last term i had faled all my classis even jim. how cud you fale jim you might be thinkin. its cuz i don't change into my fizz ed uniform becuz when i do people start callin me things like globs of fat and when i run and start sweatin theyll be like look hes drippin oil.

i also hate the teachers becuz theyre always blamin me for stuff i dint do. i got suspindid cuz they sed i wuz sprayin lotion on peepul. 1 kid dint like it and fot me. the deans calld my mother and sed i wuz a noosinse and she wuz cryin on the fone sayin me work too hard to come to america for dis. she sed dis in her jamaican aksent and the whole offis cud hear and dat embarrissd me. i hate when my mom crys cuz sumthing inside me gets really sad 2. she runs a daycare out our apartment but dont get enuff $ for the rent sumtimes so i gotta watch the kids on the weekend wile she do other jobs. im always gettin in trouble cuz i play video games or talk on the parlor fone instead and the kids bang thier heads on sumthing and start bleedin. she dint like it when i started dancin. she sed najee, are u gonna be 50 years old and dancin. i dint say nothin cuz i wuz gonna praktis every day get famis and buy her a hous cuz she workd so hard to raise me and then she wud know it wuz all worth it.

but me mookie and kowboy dint praktis cuz kowboy and me wuz always gettin suspindid.

then 1 day when we wuz all aktually in skool, we wuz talkin in the hallways.
i know a friend who hits trains, mookie sed.
so what, kowboy sed.
i told him we wuznt makin $ and he sed becuz we wuz doin it all rong.
we dint make any money cuz we wuz bein a bunch of pussys, kowboy sed.
whatever, mookie sed. he told us to meet him at union square. u comin or not?

we went to union square that day.

i wuz like omg look at all these kids!!! they must of been like hunnits of them. all in crews. all in crews. sum of them had thier crews name on thier sneakers sum of them had skullies on diffrint colors. i wuz the fattest but defnetly not the shortest 1 there. there wuz a kid 9 years old poppin and lockin and there wuz a couple of cute gurls too. every1 wuz dancin on the park steps tryna get $ from the tourests. we finely seen mookies fren. he wuz wearin a purple hoodie and his high top sed swag at the back. he seen mookie on the steps and came up 2 him.

he wuz like, like i said yall wuz doin it all rong. kowboy got offindid but then startd lissenin. mookies fren sed go 2 the L train cuz that train is wide and it go from manhattan to willyamsburg so you know theres $ at every stop. but that dont mean shit if you dont make everything a show and stick to the script.

mookie sed aight bet kowboy sed bet. i sed bet and we went to da L train.

on the L train at 14th da crowd wuz medium. kowboy steppd up cuz hes good at these things. he shoutd showtime everybody showtime! get ready for the livest show on earf. thats the script mookies fren wuz talkin about. i always heard other boys sayin that on the train but i thot they made it up themselvs and every1 made up the same thing at the same time. anyways mookie put on the stirio. i wuz nervis but i startd dancin. i wuz harlem shakin and snappin my fingers and cuppin my hands and doin the aunt jackie.

kowboy wuz like, ah get it get it get it peepul this is not easy like mookies fren sed to do. peepul still dint look. then the musik sed if thats your man then tag him in and i taggd mookie and mookie went bonkers. he climbd up on the train poles and spinnt and held on to it and movd his feet like he wuz walkin down the stairs. a couple of people wuz smilin.

kowboy yelld, we aksept $, visa, ebt foodstamps, and pichers of ur wife.
people wuz laffin and when mookie came round with the hat two ladies put somethin in.

it wuz 3 hole dollas! 1 for each of us! mookie had the hat and kep feelin the bills like they wuznt really there. we gave each other dap.

we wuz dum happy. then kowboy sed snatchies and tryed to grab the hat but it fell on the floor. then kowboy pickd it up and i sed snatchies. it wuz a joke and kowboy sed, najee y ur bum ass tryin to do everything i do. it wuz a joke but i shud of never followed kowboy. when he sed snatchies i shud of sed kowboy dont play around like that i shud of i shud of i shud of i shud of i shud of.

we went back to union square to show mookies fren the $ we had made. this wuz in front of the best buy and that big sign with the #s changin evry second. all the teams wuz takin thier gloves off and countin thier guap. mookie put his hand out ready to get sum props. but mookies fren sed guess u dont have enuff for 2nites event.

kowboy sed what evint.

the evint at 42nd.

kowboy sed, whatever and mookies fren sed, y u think we do this 4 idiot? theres an evint evry weekend.

they do it in a real dance stoodyo and they be videotapin google niceguy or mr snazzy. all the lejinds be there. u cud get notisd and blow up.

wen we herd dat we sed dats it we wanna be starz.

if u sed najee u cud be rich and famis id be hype as hell but if i had to choose i wud choose rich becuz i wud buy my mother the hous that dwyane wade has. when he retires and gos broke and sells it i wud buy it. then she wudnt have to wurry about affordin rents and livin in the same place she got a daycare. all those colors and all those toys skatterd around can be depressin sumtimes. she sed b4 i wuz born and when my father wuz alive and when she wuz in america for the 1st time she workd for rich white folks in midtown takin care of thier babies. she sed rich people live like a dream and she thot all of america wuz gonna be like that. the black people parts too. she wuz rong but i wuz gonna make her dreams come tru. i got into lite feet for all the wrong reezins i seen the kids on the train put thier cap on thier foot and flip it up on thier head and i sed i wanna flip my cap on my head with my foot too. i had no idear u cud make a livin off dis. i talkd about it with this gurl from banneker i go with named kandese.

we dint get in the evint that nite. mookie and kowboy used thier $ to buy nuggits and frys at burger king. i sed i wuznt hungry and put mine in a tin jar that i wuz gonna give my mother for the rent as soon as it got to 1 hunnit dollars.

we kep praktissin and praktissin. mookie bein the best dancer tryed to teach us how to hang upside down on the poles. i tryed to but blood kep rushin down to my head and i had to hop off. kowboy aint fleksibul either becuz he smokes too much weed and he sed eff that i'll stick to clappin and hat tricks.

ay dawan passd us in the hall in skool the next day.
my cousin seen y'all dancin in the train. that wuz y'all?
why u care so much, kowboy sed.
that wuz yall?
it wuz, kowboy sed. so what.

by lunch time every1 wuz like y'all the ones dancin on the trains cuz ay dawan is worser than a bullhorn when u tell him somethin.

dis boy from the other grade seven whose afro pick always be fallin out of his hair came 2 us where the bad kids be sittin under the black history month mural that ms. dallas did and gave us dap. he dint say nothin else. this other gurl shard her free free (thats what we call our skool lunch). it wuz frozen peeches but it tastd all rite that day. when that gurl gave us the free free kowboy stood up on one of the binches and sed we run this skool! i went home and praktissd for like six hours that day.

things wer lookin up then they had calld my mother to the skool for a meetin. i thot it wuz the usool meetin where the principle says najee ur grades arent cuttin it and do u want a job when u grow up. i walkd in the confrinse room and i seen my mother and i seen mookie there with u. u pointed me out and sed, thats the boy thats the boy.

i dont want him hangin out w/ my son.
no fi point your hand at me son like that, my own mother sed.
lets handle this profeshnly, the principle sed.
my son has been sneakin out the house to dance on the train.
mookie is easily distraktd. this boy here is the reason mookie doesnt have his head in the books.
mookie wuz kwiet.
lies, my mother sed. if me no proper lady me fi buss your face.

the room wuz hot and my cheek wuz ticklin me but i dint want to scratch it. ms. singleton, you wuz wearin a dress that wuz white and had roses on it and you wuz rockin back and forth like if u heard a peep out of me you wuz gonna sit on me and squash me. the principle wuz in the middle and she sed, were gonna deal with this. were gonna split all those boys up thank u for comin, ms. singleton.

u tappd the side of the table mookie wuz sittin and aksd mookie if he wuz gonna stay away from these boyz and mookie sed yes.

i told kowboy and kowboy sed the principle cud suck his left nut.

i told this teacher i talk 2 sumtimes (his name is nyim muhammad its muslim i googld it). he sed lite feet reminds him of break dancin an elamint of hip hop and im part of a tradishun. he also sed, i know mookie is your boy, but u hav 2 lissen 2 whateva the adults say.

the only reason i come to skool wuz becuz of kowboy and mookie. i used 2 skip. i wud come second period and put a arizona bottle by the back door and leave and come back 9th period for my alibye.

that friday when the principle put us all in diffrint classes i got home and my mother wuz sittin in the parla with a letter. she wuz sittin there silent alive but u wud of thot she wuz dead cuz when i got there she let the paper fall and i seen the paper whut it sed. the kids in the daycare wuz around runnin a muck hittin each other over the head with tonka trucks. 1 kid wuz scratchin the blue paint my mother put up.

whuts rong i sed to my mother but i knew what it wuz about the rint.

u dont worry about it najee, she sed.

no ma ill listen, i sed.

i knew some of this wuz my fault. she always scoldin me not to use the parlor phone because her clients call. but do i listen? no she lost 3 clients becuz the line wuz busy when they calld to make shur everything wuz ok. also i shud of stayed with the kids when she askd so she cud do another job that has more income. i'm a screw up and a falyure whos only good at makin fun of kids at sojourner truth until i get suspindid and then i become a falyure at everything and it makes me so sad. every person is supposd to be good at somethin.

so i'm sayin i snuck out to the trains that last time not because i'm a noosince or the bad seed. i had to show my mother that i cud be the man of the house and pay bills. i had to show her that i'm not here to fale everything. me mookie and kowboy went a hole week without seein each other and you dint let mookie out the house. thats why we snuck out.

kowboy had textd me, meet me by the square on 125th and i did.

we wuz chillin on the concrete binches where the adam clayton buildin for all the governmint people is and where they have the african festivals where they be dressin up in straw and black masks and they be dancin 2 drums. all the stores the old navy, the champions, the gaps wuz closd and the metal gates and big locks wuz over them. it wuz cold. the cold had foold me cuz it wuz hot earlier and the wind wuz blowin little peses of trash in my face. it wuz nothin but green and yellow cabs on the street makin no noise and 1 or 2 people wuz on the sidewalk by theyselvs walkin fast. it wuz times like that i be like wow the avenoo is so wide and the buildins is so tall.

kowboy sed, you and me can still make it into tonites evint.

he seent i wuznt into it and he wuz chewin a mint stick and spittin on the ground to make it a point but to me it wuz all this spit on the ground for no reason. he wuz huggin the boom box and wuz wearin his retro air force 1s.

i sed we shud of never had dreams and kowboy sed what the eff do you mean by that bro and i sed i mean we shud of never wantd 2 be stars, i sed and he sed son u sound like the people in the movies who dont beleve.

then he sed, look dude if u gettin on this train with me dont come on with that imma slit my wrist shit.

i got up but i made it look like i only got up cuz my butt wuz tired. i wuz poutin and walkin slow. the wind wuz so cold it made me wanna be home takin a warm pee. somethin sed we shudnt had been out here. all the brownstones turnt out they lights and if u got shot or abdukted nobody cud witness cuz nobody wuz out sellin incense who cud hear you scream over the street sweeper truck. there wuz one guy comin up the block and his knuckles were movin crazy like he wuz gonna punch the next person he see in the face. he wuz gray like his face and his cloths and the sidewalk wuz all the same thing.

yo son whos that, kowboy sed tryin to act macho but his voice had shakes in it.

It wuz mookie it wuz mookie it wuz mookie!

he wuz like a ghost. he had his hat on bakwards and his sneaker lases out and he wuz jumpin up and down like lets do dis. the clothes that lookd gray wuz his sweatpants with a picher of tweety bird on it. and his cutoff shirt showed his muscles but they wuz kids mussels not kriminel muscles. all this funk liftd from me and i didnt care that i wuz in the middle of the street and my mother dint know where the hell i wuz. it wuz so late that no busses had old lady passinjers only weirdos and all the white people went back to thier nice homs and all the dudes wearin bow ties took thier newspapers and went home. when mookie surprisd us it wuz like we wuzn't goin to the train platform. it wuz like we wuz goin to da beech.

its like midnight mookie, kowboy sed.
so, sed mookie.
wuznt u sposd to be on punishmint, kowboy sed.
so, sed mookie.
whatever, lets hit a train, kowboy sed.
lets hit a train, i sed.
what train we hittin, najee, kowboy sed to me.
i dont know, i sed.
thats right cuz u dont do no thinkin for yourself, u stupid ass koala bear.
it wuz a joke but it hurt.
we hittin the 2 train all the way to brooklyn, kowboy sed.

mookie stoppd him and sed, but remember what my boy sed about the L train.

the L train can fondle my scrotum, kowboy sed. this our last time we stayin on our home train.

at 116th kowboy clickd the stirio and sed, what time is it and we sed showtime. there wuz some people on the train but not that many. like five people dug in thier bags for their phones like they wuz all about to play one group game of angry birds. the train blacked out for a minute and when the lights flicked on it wuz us aginst the whole train. its hard to dance for people not enjoyin themselvs. u dont get the energy and clappin stuff like that and even if the passengers is into it they wanna act like the book theyre readin is more interestin than us. then it be embarrassin u be dancin and bendin ur elbows and shufflin and u be feelin like a fool a big fool.

it felt like that and after kowboy sed, its not illegal to show us love but nobody clappd and i dint know silence cud be like daggers. one young spanish guy with a nice goatee gave us fifty cents but he flung it to us b4 we got all the way to his side. i wantd to take those coins and fling it back at him so the metal wud hurt his face. i wantd to cuss out every1 in there. i hopd thier family died and thier hands wud b in thier face like y and id pat them on the shulder and be like now look who needs charitee.

we all got off deep in brooklyn at franklin and switchd back to the uptown train to go all the way home. the heater wuznt workin in the part of the train we went. we wuz so thirsty to get back to harlem nun of us sat down and the seats wuz paintd red and orange and faded like all the seats on the 2 train. the scrapes on them wuz also scrapes on my heart. the train wuz zoomin fast and all u seen outside of it wuz tunnels and blackness and i kept lookin out dere for somethin to tell me this wuz not my life. it went to eastern parkway grand army plaza bergen atlantic avenue up back in 2 manhattan. it got all the way to 34th street and the doors wudnt shut.

now this train dont wanna fuckin move, kowboy sed.

mookie held on to the pole in his own world.

then a mob of people wuz floodin into the train. the doors opend and closd and opend and closd and opend and when itd be about to clos someone wud stick thier hand in and it wud open up and five vulchers wud rush in.

i hate the mta i swear to god, kowboy sed and bangd the window behind them real hard.

but there wuz somethin diffrint about these people. they wuz mostly white and they wuz all in conversashuns. usually every1 be on the train sittin and standin and all u can hear is the music from one persons headphones. or every1 be on the train so close together that they cud be about to kiss and still no 1 will say nothin. but these people wuz chattin it up and laffin and bein obnokshus and some holdin brown paper bags with beverages in them. the beads on the girls necks wuz clinkin and eyeliner wuz around all of thier eyes and the dudes voices wuz so loud they sounded like engines. one guy clappd the seelin of the train and yelld, one game at a time!

and i startd noticin a lot the bodies on the train wuz rockin blue and orange and white and thier shirts had the same basketball logo on them. and kowboy wuz smilin and rubbin his hands together. why wuz he doin all that when his face wuz tight a minute ago. they were comin from a knicks game and the knicks had won. this 1 group wuz singin just a small town girl livin in a lonely world and everybody in the group knew the words.

the guy who clappd the seelin wobbld over to us his eyes lookd like they wuz filled with clear liquor and breath smellt like a hot sharp whistle. he bumpd on the train pole and the train pole bouncd him up on us and mookie cot him. and his face dartd from me to mookie to kowboy.

bro what are u doin out so late, he sed to me.
were dancers, mookie spoke up 4 me.
dude youre fuckin 8 years old.
we do dis all the time, mookie sed.
i bet u guys dont have pubic hair.

kowboy wuz still cheesin hard. i dont no why wuz he changin his mood like this. is he messin with us? i dint know why he wuz so jolly until the guy sed well show us some moves and kowboy had already turnt up the stirio.

what time is it? showtime! mookie shoutd and everybody on the train made space for us.

when they made space for us we wuz in a warm and fuzzy bubble and thats when i wuz like we got dis we got dis we got dis.

me and mookie took kowboys q and i got in.

i startd two steppin and movin my arms and the music wuz like a breeze like i wuz listenin 2 hip hop and playin gameboy at the same time. i dint have 2 pretend i wuz havin fun cuz i wuz. i actd like i threw a bomb and i snappd when it fell on the floor. i spinnd and only stoppd on the beat and kris krossd my legs and unkrossd them agin. it took a lot of effit. cute ladies pausd thier conversations and wuz watchin me. watchin me! they wuz feelin me. i wonderd if they cud see i wuz fat. i taggd mookie and dats when everybody went bananas. he hoistd himself up and b4 u new it both of his legs wuz on the higher pole and he wuz upside down and stayed like that for like ten seconds. the audeens sed ooooooh. he did three flips while the train wuz goin full speed and on 3rd one he gave this man who sittin with a grocery bag and roses stickin out dap and sniffd the flowers. you cud see his pecs workin every time he twistd his body. the train wuz like a trampoline to him. he cud bounce everywhere and land on his feet. he wuz better than the akrobats at the circus and he had rithim. his arms and legs wuz dancin like soul chicken wings and that wuz my own fren who wuz doin that. ahh ahh ahh, kowboy wuz hypin every move like that. it wuz so loud it wuz like he wuz shoutin off a cliff. these tourests in sunglasses took out their camra fones and tapd us then every1 took out thier camra fones and tapd us. it felt like we wuz on the floor of maddison square.

this one old white guy at the end wuz mesmrizd by us the hole time. his buttons on his soot wuz glintin. the collar wuz too crispy for the train. i seen him out the corna of my eye and my 1st thot wuz this man must brush his teeth with a special toothbrush. but he wuz feelin us. thats our show, mookie sed to everybody. catch us wurld wide. he cudn't go anywhere without sum1 tappin his shulder to put $ in the hat. the old man flaggd kowboy and put somethin crumpld in it. we wuz at 96th street and the train wuz zoomin past 110th and we wuz still collectin $ and when people wuznt givin us $ they touchd our elbows and sed hey that wuz good and we had to pretend like hearin that wuz as good as gettin $ which it almost wuz. we got off at 125th and i cudnt wait 2 count it all. we let the hole train leave the stashun.

thats how you fuckin hit trains, kowboy sed.
we offishul, sed mookie.
we thot we wuz done and we had to retire, i sed.
word, sed kowboy.

it wuz the first time kowboy agreed with anything i sed. mookie buttd in.

lets count this money shall we.

kowboy held it out and mookie did the tally. 1 dollar 2 dollar 3 4
5 6 7 8 9 10 11 12 13 14 15 16 dollars.

we in the evint! we in the evint!
mookie sed imma show this to my boy and be like i dare y'all not
to let us in. pladow. imma be like all y'all can pay in coins if you
want but we pay in bills 1 2 3 4—
1 of the bills wuz still crumpld up.
what's this 1, mookie sed, rollin it in his fingers.
he uncrumpld it and it wuz a bill but it wuznt gorge washington.
the number wuz weird too. it sed 100 instead of 1. we dint believe
mookie. he sed again look at dis. and it wuz real cuz you cud see
the strip in the light. that old white man gave us a hunnit dollas!

we in the evint tonite, kowboy screamd hurtin his throat.
we in the evint!

i wuz jumpn kowboy wuz jumpn mookie wuz jumpn. kowboy
tied all the money in a black plastic bag. we wuz giddy. we wuz
shinin like the lite on the train platform. the gray water drippin in
a puddle and pijjons sippin it up next to us wuz nasty but if that
wuz clean water i wud splash in it seven times over. every nite i be
up thinkin what wud of happend if everything stoppd rite there.
it wud of been the happyest nite of my life i tell u that.

but instead i dont know whut wuz goin thru my head. i do know
what wuz goin thru my head. i wuz thinkin this is a good nite to
not be the yungest no more. this is a good nite to be the 1st to
make a joke and make my frens laff and not be accusd of followin

kowboy. thats what wuz goin on but it wuznt clear like that when it wuz happenin.

what happend wuz i sed snatchies and tryed 2 seeze the bag from kowboy but kowboy got cot off guard and he droppd the bag and it fell into the tracks. it got quiet and i cud tell kowboy wuz heatd cuz mussels startd appearin in his cheeks and when that happend i got ready for what wuz next.

this fuckin idiot box, kowboy sed. see what he did.
everybody in the stations eyes wuz on me burnin my back.
what r u waitin 4 dummy go down and pick it up, kowboy sed, shovin me.
i dint like him talkin 2 me like that espeshly in front of bystanders and i figured i better stand up for myself now or never.
no, i sed to kowboy.
what u mean no. u knockd it out my hand like an ignoramus now go down and get our money.
im not goin in those tracks get it urself, i sed.
i cant believe u rite now. u better go down and get it rite now.
u get it, i sed.
son, if u dont go down and get it, u owe me 100 dollars strate up.
i wudnt go. somethin wudnt let me go. but if i dint go kowboy wuz gonna punch me. i cud feel it. i knew it wuz gonna happen defnetly. the only thing i dint know wuz if i wuz gonna cry.

i'll go get it.
it wuz mookie.

it aint no big deal. imma hop down and get it so you two nutsacks can shut up.

the words wuz formin in my mouth. forget it, mookie, leeve it there but they dint come out. maybe kowboy wuz gonna say what i cudnt and be like stop leeve it we'll ask an mta worker but there wuz no mta worker in site and kowboy wuznt budgin at all. i dint say nothin further but the electronic sign above us sed 3 minits til the next train. i wuz scard but i thot 3 minits thats plenty of time. mookie is fast and athlitik.

i'm sorry ms. singleton i'm sorry i'm sorry.

i know you think i wuz a bad inflinse on him but i wuznt i swear. i luvd him like a brother. when me and kowboy tryed to see him and u sed no i cryed all the way home. we dint go cuz we dint want to disrispeck u. we went after the hole thing wuz ova. we snuck in at midnite. kowboy brung his stirio we played it 4 mookie. i left sneakers there.

ms. singleton, please please understand that im kwittin lite feet and not dancin nemore. i'm ritin cuz i cant sleep i keep thinkin about ur son and i'm gonna rite til deres nothin lef in dis hole notebook. my mother wont speak to me she sed i done really messed up and that she dint come all the way from the caribbean 4 dis. so i'm kwittin lite feet and i'm gonna fokus on skool cuz no way i shud be readin at a third grade level. me and kowboy are gonna start by doin good in class. all 4 mookies memry. education is important its a must. pleeze reply to dis, u can yell at me, u can yoos cuss words i desurv ne punishment pleeze rite sumthin bak instted of nothin and 1 more thing i pramis i'm gonna make it up to u. when i become a rich vetanerian and after i help my mom pay her bills i'll give you all the $.

cuz I shud of—

Tumble

Usually, they give you time. You might see a notice on someone's door for the whole year. Now, several units were getting one on the same day.

So less than a week into my time as a building liaison, Emeraldine hands me a printout of Banneker tenants who got notices in the past month—twentysome in all. She does it with this attitude like she's waiting for me to object, but I just take the list and act like the new worker who's happy to get work.

We gonna start setting those folks up with the Citizens Legal Fund, she goes.

I hold up the list doing my best to murmur the names. Michelle Sutton, Darius Kite, Verona Dallas. Then I get to one that cold knocks me out. I move it close to my face to make sure it's not a mistake. Kya Rhodes.

Ever since I quit school and came back Emeraldine's been constantly on me. Everybody's supposed to be like her, gung ho for change. She thinks I threw everything away.

I didn't even wanna work for the Committee of Concern. I wanted to work for a magazine, interviewing celebrities, but every magazine from Fifth to Eighth Avenues treated my résumé like it was invisible. If I hadn't seen the clipping in the lobby, I would have had to cut my losses and been a Macy's perfume girl.

So now I'm fielding phone requests. I'm cleaning out the communal fridge. I never thought I'd be stuck working with three old ladies. One who thinks she's Cleopatra and is always looking at me over her glasses.

I was a division one gymnast and now I'm back living with my parents. I already feel like a disappointment. But this Kya thing seriously paralyzes me.

Emeraldine and Corinthia said she was holding on by one tooth. That they saw her at the Dunkin' Donuts begging the cashiers not to throw out the leftovers. That her mother died and left her with a hefty casket price. I should be empathizing but I was tuning out. I can only concentrate on how it's been two years since I saw her, and the last time wasn't good.

That Sunday after I got the list, we throw a luau-themed cookout in the back of the building to calm tenants down about all the evictions. Our building got sold to new owners, so now all our places are basically being prepared to become deluxe apartments in the sky. All of a sudden, you look next door and a wreath you've seen all your life is gone. People haven't been taking it well. Lots of loud last parties. Lots of slanted box springs in the hallway. Not too long ago someone lit a ball of yarn on fire in the laundry room. I don't blame them. That kinda thing would hurt anyone's psyche.

Anyhow, I help cover the bazaar tables with plastic straw and set up the serving trays. Emeraldine and Corinthia wear hula skirts. Raspreet brings this really cool sculpted cane from her country and a ukulele. Children are rolling around all cute with their faces painted. Hot thuggish guys who would ruin my life are sitting on lawn chairs in socks and Nike sandals. Somebody brings their boom box. Everyone's enjoying the food and the breeze.

It feels like people are staring at me, and it's not because I'm a grown woman and I'm tiny. I'm already used to everyone thinking I talk white.

The whole time it feels like there's a girl with over-Vaselined lips waiting to pounce on me.

I actually call in sick the Monday after the luau cookout and stay upstairs. I grew up in this apartment with my mom, dad, brother Timmhotep, and Rerun, our female shih tzu. My parents were Black Panther sympathizers and gave me the name Quanneisha because they felt it was strong and powerful. I shortened it of course. My mom does janitorial work at the Sydenham clinic and my dad has a table on Adam Clayton where he sells incense and sometimes phone cards.

Taking the day off is dicey because my parents weren't thrilled about me dropping out in the first place and said I could only stay if I kept business hours. Ma's not home because they needed an extra person at the hospital to mop the labs. With my brother still in Arizona, I can put the divider sheet up and have both sides of the room. I wait for my dad to leave, so it could just be me, Rerun, and her slobber.

But that doesn't work because right when my dad is heading out to set up his stand, he gives me one of his looks and goes, You been takin Rerun out?

I have been, I say. I do it real early in the morning and real late at night.

What about your friends from school? You see any of them yet? Not yet.

For a second, he is about to dwell on it, but decides against it and undoes the door chain.

Well, don't stay in here all day, he goes. There's a world out there just waitin on you.

I try to say, Hey, Neish, you're a tough girl. I was tough since the day I knew I wanted to be a gymnast when I saw Kerri Strug on TV. I thought it was so awesome how she lifted her hands to the sky like, hey everybody, come hug me. I was eight years old. That same afternoon, I backflipped off this broken slide and landed on my feet. I wish I could say that's all she wrote, but you just don't hop around in a playground in Harlem and ta-da. Nobody's gonna go, Look at little Neisha, let's nurture her. When I saw that flyer at the Central Park Zoo that said Come one, come all, tumble away, I literally had to snag it down before my teacher reported me missing. I remember the night I showed it to my mother who wasn't against slapping the foolishness out of anyone.

Oh no. Not gonna happen, sweetie.

You don't know what it's about!

I don't know what it's about, she said, but I know how much it costs.

That would have been the end of that had she not seen the line my brother scribbled at the bottom which was: she get to do backflips with rich girls. My brother who you only heard when his Sega Genesis was overheating.

My mother finally relented, and I wound up at a gym in Midtown with all these girls in polka-dot and neon leotards, and me in jean shorts. Straddling the uneven bar for dear life until I hear my shorts tear. I had to be tough. Everybody thinks you'll automatically become that Black girl who's the best. But you really have to watch out because otherwise, you might be that urban girl who tries to hang, gets over her head, and quits.

I only ever invited Kya to a meet once when we both were around ten. We were only three months apart in age. She was in the courtyard one day in kindergarten and our mothers basically shoved us forward to shake hands. It was awkward because just seconds ago, her mother was cussing her out. Normally, my parents would call that a red flag, but we were the only two children out that day, and it would have been kinda rude not to say hi. From there, we ran into her and her mother coming from the 2 train. Every summer next to the jungle gym and sand the homeless people peed in, we'd parlay while my mother watched me from the lobby window. I'd do a somersault for Kya and she'd say, Whoo! Wow! And you not even afraid of falling!

I spent most my time training and at a prep school one of the dads at Midtown Gymnastics helped me get into, in other words not around Black people. I was fascinated with Kya, how even in the fifth grade her voice sounded like it was filled with concrete. How Ashanti would come on out someone's window, and she would start dancing lazily and effortless, like she was possessed by a rhythm she didn't even want.

I trained six days a week, six hours a day for eight years straight. I was constantly taping myself up and falling these ghastly falls. Some days I felt like I couldn't even move. Some days, I felt like an absolute beginner. I hardly focused on school. I killed my body. I spent a good part of my life in tears. But I fought through it. I ate my soy and listened to my Ramones. That's what I did all of high school and it paid off.

I was in the student lounge at school the day a local magazine announced I was invited to Nationals. At Banneker, they hung a banner from the front wall of the bingo room. Somebody from the public access channel came by and interviewed me. Tenants kept asking me for photos and to backflip.

Kya, on the other hand, was up to smoking Newports and wearing expensive blouses that still had the tags on them. Her crowd was seedy, but she always said that they were just her friends and she wasn't like them. That week that the building put the banner up for me, she hung with a bunch of other teens in black bandannas out back by the dumpsters on beat-up lawn chairs drinking and slap boxing. They knew about me. They saw the banner. But they were fine in their little underworld. One evening, I saw them out there sitting on each other's laps and I decided to take out the garbage. I had my headphones in and kept my head up like I couldn't be bothered, but as I passed by them, I accidentally smeared my garbage bag on somebody's Nikes.

I'm sorry about that, I said.

It was really quiet, but then as I continued, I heard someone repeat, I'm sorry about that, followed by Kya busting out in giggles. It was the giggles that struck me down.

So I said fine.

The very next day I wore a hoodie that the Nationals' press office sent me. It was eighty-five degrees, but I wore it anyway. Anytime I was in the lobby and any of them was in earshot, I made it a point to use big words. If I was posing for a picture with somebody and one of them was behind me, I'd take my sweet time.

Then Kya's boyfriend kissed me. I swear I didn't ask for that. He taps me on the arm in the elevator when I'm minding my business and goes, You that acrobat girl, and I go, You mean gymnastics, and he goes, Bet you be doing that stuff naked, and right in the middle of me telling him and his boy I wasn't the one, he kisses me, which of course gets back to Kya's ears as the other way around.

Two weeks before Nationals, I go to take Rerun for a walk out of the back entrance at night. I bend down to fix her collar and when I get up I'm surrounded by a whole bunch of black bandannas. Kya is in the background. Her friend Princess gets in my face and goes, So you wanna mess with people's mans? then knees me in the gut.

They're kicking and punching, but then they grab hold of my hoodie and start pulling it off. Once they did that, one of the girls takes it to this parked car and wraps it in the axle like it's some rag and when it's nice and dirty one of the boys throws it on the floor, takes out his penis, and pisses on it. I'm 100 percent sure they would have picked it back up and thrown it on me had a woman not walked by and yelled, What's going on over there?

The very next evening, I'm back at their little dumpster den and flanked beside me are two cops. There they are, I go, looking everybody in the eye. I look Kya in the eye the longest. It's not until the handcuffs come out that she realizes what's going on.

I'm a teenager, she blurts out. Please!

The last scream is so shrill, it vibrates my ribs. I was this close to telling the cops never mind. But I didn't. Her eyes were violent and dead. It should have satisfied me, but it did nothing. I had a muscle contusion and fractured wrist. I tried to continue training for Nationals, but I couldn't get through any of my routines. The day I withdrew my name, I sobbed all night. My teammates tried to cheer me up. You'll get another chance, they said, but I was seventeen. As I powdered up for my Michigan meets that fall semester, I told myself, Neish, look where you made it all the way to. A free education. Those crowds would be blazing with spirit, but I could only concentrate on the empty seats and half-assed it. Right before our northwest showcase, I quit. I walked the campus the whole next year as an ex-gymnast. Then I quit school altogether.

Work with the committee drags on for about a week until the town hall on the first Wednesday of the month. Usually, the town halls are about repairs or pests or mail getting put in the wrong slot, but the last time the evictions hogged the show. They had to start moving the meetings to the Y on 135th because people were on top of each other.

You owe it to yourselves! Emeraldine starts her speech that night in the gym to, like, a hundred tenants in grays and blacks. Why are you suffering on an island? Why are you letting your landlord win? You wanna be sweet-talked? You wanna be slapped around with hikes?

She gestures with her chin for me to usher the standing guests into seats, but I ignore her.

I don't get a joy of saying I told you so, she continues. I don't get a joy out of seeing you kicked out. I don't get a joy out of seeing you get washed away. Not when that same wave's coming for me, too. But we're working for you. See that young lady back there. Remember Neisha Miles? Well, she's back and I'm gonna have her go door-to-door and set up anyone in danger of eviction with a free lawyer. You'll be seeing her face a lot. All you have to do is trust us.

Everybody turns to look back at me. All I hear is chairs, and I'm seething.

After the whole thing is over and she's patted everybody on the back for coming from work and has kissed all the babies, Emeraldine pokes my shoulders hard while I'm unplugging the sound system and goes, Are you ready for this mission?

I'm thinking, To help the girl who cost me a shot at being a professional? The girl who would probably attack me? No. I almost ask to trade her with someone else, if it didn't mean she'd probably get helped.

I half nod.

For the next two days, I print tenants' rights leaflets. I reach out to the *Amsterdam News*. I organize the office and field phone requests. I write down the logistics for a flea market that isn't supposed to happen until the end of the summer. I flyer the bulletin board.

During idle moments, I look up schools in New York. I think about my future. I always thought I'd be an Olympian, but obviously that's not possible anymore. I think maybe I could be something cool like the executive director of the Miss America pageants. In high school, I got B pluses. I wasn't the queen of work ethic, but I wasn't a goof. Anyhow, I find a list of CUNYs and have a mild interest in a couple of them, but with no scholarship I would have to pay out of my own pocket.

I tell myself that I have no choice but to concentrate on this job until I get my act together. In the meantime, I pretend that the list is a mistake and Kya isn't really here.

I step outside one night to meet some friends for drinks and I see a girl in the courtyard. I recognize her in a jiffy and there goes the Kya-not-being-here fantasy.

She has on this velour tracksuit that's worn down and she's in the company of these thuggish guys. She might have gained weight. I can't tell. She's still cute, but her clothes are too baggy. And right there by the tree in the dirt are her kids, drawing circles.

She's having this super loud conversation.

She's like, I told him, Get these shits out my face. All these shits is blurry! That nigga clumped his shits up like a blanket and was out!

Immediately I'm taken back to the days of her hanging in those lawn chairs in the back by the dumpster.

The guys start howlin. One of them goes, You should of been, like, I change my mind, give me ten of them shits! This really cracks her up, too, and sends her hopping across the pavement to a tree where the squirrels see her but continue gathering their nuts. Her kids are there and she playfully bops them and gives them a hug.

I don't know what to do. I pretend to forget something and turn on my heel back toward the building to leave out the back entrance. I think about the night she stomped me out. How afterward, she and her friends taped my buzzer down so it would ring all night. I remember how they passed me in the lobby the next day and this thin girl brushed her shoulders by me with a force from the jungle.

Why is she so animated now? Isn't her life in shambles?

When it comes time to go to Kya's apartment I decide that instead of knocking, I'll slip a generic note under her door and hope things work themselves out.

Days go by.

Corinthia, Raspreet, and I are at the table by the hanging plants, tearing raffle tickets and piling them on a drum from last year's summer gala. Corinthia loves talking about celebrities whose lives are a mess.

They catch them in the cars with hookers, she goes. Catch them in the broom closet with the maid. Committing insurance fraud. It's ridiculous. We're the ones supposed to be frauding. Not them! That's why I love me some Barack. And some Michelle. And some Serena. And some Venus. And some Flo-Jo. And some Dominique Dawes. And some— Neisha why'd you quit?

I shrug my shoulders and prepare to hear that for the rest of my life.

You must have been better than 99 percent of those girls.

But not better than 99.9, I want to say. Instead, I shrug my shoulders again.

Well, just know they not you. I don't care how many Wheaties they eat.

Yes, Raspreet says, dumping tickets in some empty Tupperware, I agree to that.

By the way, when you were doing your routines and things, did the camera ever do a close-up and your butt was ashy?

We all bust out laughing at the question and at my answer, which is yes. Emeraldine is by herself on the other side with the board games and the Magnavox. I guess us enjoying each other's company and her being alone with a stack of boxes from Trader Joe's gets to her. Like when she's by herself sometimes humming these low melodies and it looks like the weight of the world is crawling out of her fro.

All of a sudden, she comes to me and says, Neisha, can I speak to you in private?

So I just wanted to give you an update on Kya, she begins, sitting next to me. Who happens to be the only one on your list with small children. I was informed the other day that her tenancy was terminated and the building has started her lawsuit. They gave the thirty days yesterday. Someone can still represent her, but that hasn't happened because she hasn't been connected to them yet. I understand she's on your list?

Yes, but I haven't gotten around to her.

And why is that?

I've been busy.

Oh, okay. I also wanted to let you know Dayanelliz Colon reached out to me the other day saying she finished her Hostos College credits and was wondering if I had anything. I told her what I'm telling you, which is I'm gonna give you a few weeks and we'll see.

The last sentence stings me and of course everybody in the room can hear it and is pretending there's nothing in the air but air. Emeraldine gets up and the chair creaks.

I wanna tuck my head down and leave and never come back. I sit there like a scolded child and push my chair away with slow hot embarrassment. All you can hear for the rest of the day is the ceiling fan and everybody else flipping pages.

Well, what is it you wanna be then? my mother asks me later from the kitchen.

I don't know, I say. But I know this is not it.

You were a hero at sixteen when you got us that free trip to Utah and you were a hero when you got that job downstairs.

Tell that to the boys and girls at Mich who are gonna be lawyers.

Since when were we into other people's grass?

You don't understand, Ma.

Understand what?

That stuff matters with people.

Does it matter with you?

Don't make me answer that.

It's useless even bringing it up. My parents grew up in a place where a bad storm could take everything you had in a fell swoop and so they were always fine with what they had. Growing up, we ate from a table some wealthy lady gave my dad when he was a mover. My parents' idea of the ultimate fun is getting together in the living room and watching old videotapes of themselves in someone's backyard dancing to "She's a Bad Mama Jama."

I was proud of you from the third grade when you could read better than me, my dad says from the living room couch where he's got his blanket and his *Mary Tyler Moore* rerun. And I was never a slouch at reading.

Thank you, Robert, Ma says.

She scrunches up her eyebrows real serious to me and goes, What is this really about? Are you gonna tell me or do I have to spend hours reading it on your face?

She keeps staring into my eyes like an answer's gonna magically pop up. It gets so awkward that I just relent.

Emeraldine wants me to help Kya.

And?

I'm not gonna.

And why is that?

Because.

Because why?

This is all her fault.

So you want her to drown?

I don't want her to drown. I just don't want anything to do with her.

She cuts off the faucet, and there go the hurt lines running up her face.

Robert, turn that TV off a second.

Listen, love, she goes to me and I swear the whole building is quiet.

I'm with you. But let me ask you something. Is that what you're gonna let consume your life? A grudge against someone who life done gave them theirs already?

The darts are hitting my heart. I'm this close to just falling on her shoulder. Except I don't budge. I shift in my chair and look past her.

They tryna take her kids, Kya. Did you know that? She leaves the two of them by themselves while she goes to work. They're saying ACS should be around here any day. Does that make you feel any way?

Silence.

Look, I didn't say anything when you quit school. I didn't say anything after I basically begged Emeraldine to take you. I let you pave your own way. But I'm telling you this. If you're not gonna have something to do with that woman, then don't have anything to do with me because that doesn't sound like anything in my family tree.

And that's when I start spinning the rim of my coffee mug.

I had two days to report back to Emeraldine. Per her orders, I had to visit every tenant on my list. I had to make sure they had their lease, rent statements, payment receipts, and the eviction notice ready. I was supposed to put them in contact with Jamaal Wesley, and he would follow up.

Raspreet and I decide to meet in the lobby and do our names together. She comes downstairs carrying this big brown bag like she always does, full of lord knows what. She's always pausing to greet somebody and most of the time it's like awww, but when she stops this time because a woman's grocery bag spills and ends up talkin about squash, I speak up.

Raspreet, I go after holding the elevator door open the third time. Raspreet!

Huh?

Maybe we should split up and meet up afterward.

I've been to almost every floor in Banneker, but I still get nervous because they always seem darker and dimmer than mine. Like the one where someone was playing a Harry Potter movie on full blast that spooked the mess out of me.

The first door I knock on belongs to a man with a keloid under his chin. His face and the way he keeps talking as if it wasn't there stays in my head until a woman comes to the next door I knock on mixing something nasty that looks like wet oats. Then there's the dark-skinned couple from the floor below mine who both happen to be tall and magazine-spread gorgeous. On the third floor, there's a woman in her fifties named Verona.

What you say your name was again? she goes.

I'm taken aback that everything's so clean, not that I was expecting dirtiness.

Neisha.

Neisha, you talk funny.

They're all like, Thank you, thank you, thank you. Everybody I visit is like, Thank you, thank you. Even though some of them have their foreheads down.

In the hallway, Kya's name pulsates at me. For a second my teeth chatter and I say to myself, *This is ridiculous. Just walk up the stairs.* I start to stomp my way pretending to be a badass. But everything simmers to the surface again, the back lot, my predicament here, and I just can't.

· · ·

I knocked on Kya's door but nobody was there, I say when Emeraldine checks in the next day about the visits, and in this singsongy way she goes, Luckily, you got a week before Jamaal comes to town.

The following Monday, two representatives from ACS double-park their car out front and take away Kya's kids. I'm in the lobby and with a few others can see everything from the window. The little girl looks confused. Kya, surprisingly, is as calm as brushed hair until the engine starts. Then she bangs on the car window, goes, I hope you have a good rest of the day stealing people's families, and watches them pull away.

She spends the whole day outside. The next day, I see her across the street walking by this plastic bag floating in the air. Her kids aren't there, and it's like a fact she's ignoring. I know she'll get them back in a few days, but I know the eviction is next. I try to prepare myself to live with this, and stand my ground, but a thousand flies invade my heart.

After a tumultuous three weeks, Ma's fiftieth finally comes and she books the bingo room with streamers, tuna salad, and lopsided cake. She is wearing a purple Mabelina on her head with these floral clusters and ruffles and boy, is she strutting her stuff.

I try to be lively, but there's only so much revelry I can enjoy. I have a few days to finish my visits, but I'm nowhere close to doing the one that counts. I sit off to the side eating a slice of cake that I know I won't finish. Ma brings some of her friends by and when she asks if I remember them, I smile, but it's torture.

Emeraldine had invited herself to the party. At some point, she goes over to the sternos and says, Nobody touched my baked ziti? Oh hell no! Then she heads out to the entrance by the security cam to look for people who might want a plate. I know exactly what she is doing. Moments later, five people come in all humble, looking like they would leave right away if anyone gave them a sideways look. One of the stragglers is Kya Rhodes, unaware of the theater she is walking into.

By now I have seen her a few times since I have been back, but this is the first time we're in the same room with my dreams unable to protect me.

She's so out of it, I don't think she even knows whose party it is. Still, to avoid anything, I stay on the other side of the room until she makes her plate and leaves.

It isn't until Ma sashays herself upstairs and her bingo friends siphon off the last of the macaroni pie, after chairs are folded and balloons popped, tape scraped off and cloths flopped out, that my last bit of energy brings me to the elevator doors, which thank god just slide open for me. Before I can exhale, I notice a young woman in pajama pants and a New York Knicks jersey already on. It's her. Her hair is pulled taut in a bun and she's balancing a cigarette from the corner of her mouth. Nicks and bruises speckle her face. The door shuts.

Our eyes meet. I brace myself for anything. For a confrontation or worse: the smirk that tells me that she knows my life. She stands there doing nothing, but then in an instant recognizes me.

I don't know what else to do so I nod. She nods back. It's a sustained nod that shoots inside me. She knows all right. She knows all I ever aspired to be. I stay there flayed until she finally speaks up.

Your mother was in the purple hat, right?

Yes, I mumble.

I almost didn't recognize her. That was her party down there?

Yes.

She looked like she was enjoying herself.

That's all she says.

The elevator ascends during this time and opens up to Kya's floor. There she walks off as quietly as she appears. In the rush to make sense of everything, I realize I haven't hit the button to my own floor. I go to touch the twenty-one, my head still spinning, only to discover the button already pressed for me.

Federation for the Like-Minded

I knew that restaurant across the street was set to be a bane at my side from day one.

It wasn't more than a week after they did it up one of the waiters comes right out to where it's me and the pigeons and says, Sorry, I'm gonna have to ask you to leave. I don't understand what he's sayin until I catch him lookin at my chessboard and crate and for the first time since I ever been on that block I realized that I was on private property. The second I came to this, I pack everything up and says, Sir, I apologize duly, all the while wonderin how a wholesome game could be a sore sight for anyone.

You see me here. I don't bother nobody. I'm not runnin up on you and askin for your life. I'm here with my board from right when the sun wakes until it's just me and the sanitation trucks. I play anyone whether knucklehead or salesman, all in the name of brain exercise and good conversation. Wasn't any different when I was in front of that restaurant, and before that when the spot was a bodega with the deli meat the flies loved so much. I greeted the patrons comin out, asked them for a go, and enough of them said why not.

You crossed the street here yourself, and what did I tell you? That all I was out here for was fresh air and recreation? When you pulled up a chair, did I speak any evil of that place? All I said was I was glad you crossed the street and found me. That you'd take black and I'd take ivory.

I been here from jump, back when that big retail store at the bend of 125th and Frederick Douglass was a butcher shop and the fan used to blow the whiff of carved flesh out on the sidewalk. From when as kids we'd be on top of abandoned houses jumpin from one roof onto the next. I had been on that block with my board since when I came back home from the war. That was when any old car would pull up on the curb and almost bust your kneecap. When all these fronts you see around were graveyards for busted TVs and abandoned cars, and the grass, if it grew at all, grew derelict out of the concrete like trash salad. I'm not sayin this with pride. I'm sayin I had been there all that time, always treated the pigeons nice, and never once pissed on the concrete.

Anyhow, the second time the badge boys came, I had been protrudin more to the middle of the sidewalk cuz a tied-up trash bag was thrown down on the spot I usually claim. It was two hombres. They didn't make a speech, jus politely lifted me from the crate and put me in the Crown Victoria.

I says to them, I guess I'm goin with the siren boys.

And one of them says, Hey, that's Officer Friendly to you.

But this time as they were doin their dance, Miss Emeraldine from my buildin, and her troop of women friends smellin like earth soap, happened to be strollin up that side of the street. This is where the balloon busted, if you will.

The minute the one officer took hold of my bicep, those ladies stopped their wonderful afternoon and one of them steps in and says, We wouldn't be puttin old men in jail now, would we?

Just when she seen they were set to treat her like a fleck of dust, she spoke up again and said, I'm sorry, I'm Emeraldine Heard from the Banneker Terrace Committee of Concern, and that there is Corinthia and that there is Quanneisha. And you must not know how fast we write letters.

I knew about Emeraldine. She was the one who make the sternos work at the community barbecues and who on account of her associate's degree thinks she's the boss of everybody. The others I recognized from them brushin by me in the buildin all the damn time without so much as an ado includin the time I was stuck in the lobby bathroom on bated breath waitin for instructions on how to jimmy the knob.

The officer said, We got a call about loitering and we're responding to it.

And Emeraldine said, lookin cross, We don't need you up here. Y'all need to be down on Wall Street.

Sharp words were bandied back and forth, and before I knew it, Emeraldine said, How about we stand right in front of your car and see if you assault us on your way back to it.

I seen where this was goin, so I shook my arm out for a second and said, Look, here I am, and fumbled my way to the squad car my damn self.

Your move.

. . .

Not to throw subliminals, but some people say they about change when they really about rounds of applause. The photo op. Look at me helpin the down and out! Pattin someone on the head to them constitutes a whole lifetime of charity. The whole while they got talons and agendas. They talk a fair game, but I'm convinced of zero to a little bit of it.

I might just be an old man with a tough liver who has never been past 125th Street in years. The one who come out early in the mornin, and go on his walk from one end of the compound to the flowerbed near the front gate. But I stand on the shoulders of giants and I peer out at what is and what could be.

I'm not gonna deny what these ladies do. Sometimes you need somebody to come around to make sure you're still breathin. Someone to buy the Windex and wipe the scrawlin off the lobby glass. If I ignored that, I'd be nothin short of spiteful. But does that give one the right to overstep boundaries? To get bent over with power? To not leave a man alone?

After that second time with the policeman, I decided to lay low and I took to the nook in the back of Banneker near the railin that wobbles. I had it in mind if I went to that restaurant in the late afternoon with my board, I'd blend in with the crowd. Wouldn't be noticeable at all. But before I could settle in, just me and the building's shadow, those same ladies, smellin like mothballs and hair mosturizer, hunted me down, determined to kill any serenity life could offer. I heard rustlin and murmured words. There was a new lady with them whose bones was sharp and whose perfume stung my nose so hard my derriere clenched up.

Mr. Murray, Ms. Emeraldine says, this is Eunice from the *Amsterdam News*.

Before I could breathe my next breath, that gal clicked on her tape recorder and goes, Is that restaurant bullying you? and I said, No, Is that restaurant bullying you? and she says, Are the cops bullying you? and I said, Only if that's the new phrase for givin orders.

She nodded at everything I was tryin to tell her, and two weeks later, Bam, here come the paper where she wrote the story about me. "Old Man Being Forced Out of His Favorite Spot. The tenants of Banneker Terrace in Central Harlem are sticking up for a vulnerable senior's right to a city block." I swear! The daggone thing was lyin on one of the foldin chairs in the laundromat next to some magazines. It went on from there with all these scholastic words about how that restaurant was cuttin off the locals.

As if that old bodega was the good old days. What about the spoiled bread? What about everyone yellin for they change and actin like they didn't know what a line was? Or what about how those same ladies last year was at the town hall complainin about high fructose? Now, here come fine cuisine and some occasional live jazz and they wanna act like it's a fight against fascism. As if that place don't bring out nothin but fine folks like yourself.

Your move.

·   ·   ·

See, the problem is when you old, everybody think you satisfied with the livin you've done. They like to think of you as perfumed in dry piss waitin for your call to sunset. Never mind you could have a whole twenty years left. They'll still act like your back is crooked. You think I just come out here to expire?

Let me tell you suttin. I may not be the smartest in the shed, but I've got ideas. If I didn't, I wouldn't have a checkin account with Social Security in it that gives me interest every month. They don't understand that. They busy lookin at your bottom lip waitin to see dribble. They don't wanna see you steeped in glory. They want you huddled in the gutter like a footnote.

Everybody wanna focus a damn column and use it as an excuse to target a restaurant. Everybody wanna put on a pair of marchin boots and raise a bullhorn. We gonna show that restaurant what's what! Pearline on the fifth floor. Gwenita. Ms. Dallas in 3C. Philippa. The kids, their tricycles. All of them, we gonna stand up for you, Mr. Murray. Might as well been speakin Mongolian because pity, pity, pity is all I heard.

One of the tenants spotted me by the keypad downstairs, this flighty gal who always gotta tangle her arm around everybody like she and them are goin steady, said, Mr. Murray, I'm gonna make a sign that says, Hands Off Our Elders.

I said right back to her as frank as I could, Now, that would be a phenomenal waste of time.

She had the nerve to look at me like that's not what she expected.

And I stood there in that vestibule refusin to give her solace until she had no choice but to turn around and leave like a hurt cub lickin its own wounds.

Another day Emeraldine seen me try to skip by her on the way to the elevator. She gonna hook me with her gnarled nails and you know what she had the gall to say?

I see you're all wound up.

Of course, I was riled up!

I said, I don't need anybody to hold up signs for me and she looked at me like I hadn't read my history book.

See, that's why you have the debilitated climbin Mt. Everest and senators holdin on to power. Blind men tinklin piano keys and people playin guitar with their toes. That's why a quarter of the people dyin don't tell a soul. Yet walk in any buildin and you'll see somebody who can't hold a lousy door open without bowin his head in condolence.

Why can't more people be like you? From the moment I slid my pawn over, you were hell-bent on getting the best of me. See how you got my queen stuck moted on both sides where I can't go nowhere? Why can't more people be like that?

Have them tell it, they'd say Mr. Murray needed us to barge right up to that restaurant's windowpane. He needed someone to stand up to those law books and demand his rights. Who else was gonna yell for him? Poor Mr. Murray and his sad and battered life. Mind you, did they dedicate any time to the consultin of me? Did it ever come across anyone's mind that this might require my blessin? So I say, Fine, don't consult me. But don't get irate if I sit by myself and have no part of it.

My apartment is such that I can watch my shows while smellin what deliciousness the Africans is cookin across the hall. I can look out the winda and see down the avenue, and then take a warm shower and think about life for the fifteen minutes of heat it allows. My bed is low enough I can roll out of it with no injury and disappear into my own pot of coffee. I got a box fan on the sill aimed right at my favorite chair when I sit down.

So inside or outside, it don't make much a difference any way. I could stay indoors much longer than I can keep my head under-water. Wouldn't take but a switch in my head to bolt my door. Which is what I did, and I would have stayed put had it not been a few nights before when I closed my eyes and dreamt of a ghost that turnt into Mr. Benjamin Banneker himself. Go ahead and diagnose me.

Standin before me like a hologram, he said he taught hisself letters and could trace his blood back to the coast and still all he got in his name is crumblin walls. I woke up and said to myself, Ain't that a fact. Even when your name is in front of a buildin they treat you like suttin's that's never lived.

I had had enough, I tell you. Of all these so-called friends pre-tendin they knew what was in my heart and in my id. Can you picture that? Every Tom, Dick, and Janet thinkin you got nothin cuz a corner was snatched up from under you. I was gonna show them what it felt like to have all your business out there. By walkin down there and puttin everybody else's business out there. And I wasn't blinkin twice about it.

Two dozen tenants! A mob of them on a perfect summer day meant for kayakin. Standin right by the entrance to the restaurant with signs and loudspeakers. Emeraldine was there and her lackeys. Philippa, Gwenita, and a couple others who I wouldn't have known from a spot in the rug. They was actin like it was a goddamn picnic. They brought water coolers with them and chips. Even the patrons was scared to open the door because of them. Give us our sidewalks back! was what they shoutin. Respect what was here before! A block of linked arms and gruntin. The bourgies dinin by the hedges heard it all as did the gentlemen inside and the ladies with them.

I marched right up in the middle of all that. You should of seen how I had them at full attention.

I stood right in front of that entrance tent and I says, Listen up.

And here goes sorry Miss Emeraldine talkin about, Hush everybody. Mr. Murray has suttin real important to say.

I was gonna let it all spew. I was gonna call out Gwenita for claimin other people's kids, Philippa for the stuff her husband do, Ms. Dallas for her situation, everybody who seen me on the streets and seen right thru me. Then, I was gonna ask everyone out loud if they ever once, ever once stopped by me to play. I really was about do it, but then I took a look at those faces, the swarms of goodwill in them, all open like the purest of lakes, ready for me to pat them on the shoulder and let them know they done all right. I suddenly became too much of a pussyfoot to take that away.

I just wanna some my appreciation for all this, I says instead. Thank you. And I continued to be the sweet Mr. Murray everyone wanted me to be.

So they could commence to strokin each other's feathers and takin black-and-white photos. And say although they couldn't get me back on that block, they did file the ordinance in my name for this side of the street. The same one we on now.

Say, I have a favor to ask.

I feel bad comin over the hill and blindsidin you like this. I really do, but I got to before we're done here.

I know you be in that restaurant carousin with those who recognize you by name. You enjoyin the World Cup, enjoyin the election. You seem like the type who if you said suttin reasonable, the rest would break their heads noddin to it.

See that day, when all that cahootin was goin on, I didn't lack for one match the whole rest of the afternoon. It was a fine day—I mean, really fine. It was then with that little crowd around me I had a vision. All of us out there every Saturday, playin. It wouldn't be nothin fancy. You'd show up humble, play somebody to the brink, then shake hands. I even got one of the youngbloods to go to 135th Goodwill for boards, the boards you see under me now.

Let me just come out with it: the bus don't let out on this side. Of the hundreds who empty that restaurant every day, you bout one of the only few who ever thought to cross the street.

Next time you in there with your buddies drinkin a glass of the finest, could you lean in and ask them what they got goin on in the way of recreation? If they enjoy things that work the brain and open the heart? If yes, tell them to cross the street and check me out. They wouldn't be sorry they did.

Anyhow, regardless of how this goes, grateful for the time. This sure is a beautiful city, isn't it? Don't worry, I can carry everything back with me. See the boards stack in the crate like this, the table folds up, and the legs guide me home. Anyhow, promise me you'll do what I said. Weekdays, after sundown you hear? And Saturdays past noon. I'll be right here.

Acknowledgments

Cheers

To Lorrie Moore, Adam Ross, and Ethan Bassoff. This book would not exist without you. I cannot repay you for your immense help and support.

To my family. My mom, Fatima Fofana; my sister Seree Fofana and my brother Abdul Fofana; Uncle Ismaila; Uncle Mohammed; my cousin Fatima; my dad; Aunty Anifah, love you all.

To my dear Lindsay, and my son, Dante, who is only five. *By the time I do this mix he'll probably be six.*

To Lynne "Mama" Strachan and James "Papa" Strachan.

To the Griot: Noah Barnes, Jude Somefun, Andrew Belton, and Ben Becker, my best friends for life.

To my editor, Kathy Belden, for her nurturing, steady hand.

To Rebekah Jett, for her editorial guidance. To the wonderful team at Scribner: Nan Graham, Jason Chappell, Zoey Cole, Clare Maurer, and Mark Galarrita. They are the reason this book is in your possession.

To Gabriel Louis, who has been in this writing life with me from day one.

To fellow creator Oliver Munday.

ACKNOWLEDGMENTS

To my students past and present at Frederick Douglass Academy VII and the Brooklyn School for Math and Research. You inspire me with your uniqueness and creativity.

To my fellow educators Dr. Perry Rainey, David Hobgood, Deanna Torres, Stacey Morrison, Carolyn Mathurin, Padma Paramanada, Littleton Scott, Candice Simmons, Vanessa Deravin, Jacintha Mondesir, Michele Carmargo, Chris Arroyo, Suraiyah Abdul Wahab, Vinnessa Coles, Tamika Matheson, Eric Jordan, and so many others. To all the school teachers worldwide.

To the Virginia Center for Creative Arts, Bread Loaf, and the Center for Fiction. In particular, Thierry Kehou, Sara Batkie, and Linda Morgan. To my fellow fellows including Chantal Johnson, Diane Chang, and Kimberly Coleman Foote, whose books I'll be hopefully reading soon.

To Brigid Hughes, Megan Cummins, Laura Preston, and Sarah Blakley-Cartwright at *A Public Space* for all the years of warmth.

To Alec Hill, Annie Adams, and Eric Smith at the *Sewanee Review*.

To *Granta*.

To the Admirals Writing Group: J. T. Price, Zack Graham, Cecile Berberat, Ashley Taylor, Anna Schwartzman, Dolan Morgan, Conor Martin, Simona Blat, Ryan Boyle, Nicole Starczak, and Yoojin Na, for your key feedback on many of these stories.

To Laura Isaacman for your guidance.

To the Waverly Writing Group: Kate Uraneck, Tina Nelson, Susan Lee, and Nathalie Le Du.

To the fabulous writers Ayana Mathis, Ben Fountain, Mitchell Jackson, and Justin Taylor for your many encouraging words.

ACKNOWLEDGMENTS

To my NYU professors Chuck Wachtel, Darin Strauss, Rick Moody, and Brian Morton. To my fellow NYU writers Jakki Kerubo, Adam Dalva, Christopher Foo, Dinika Amaral, Jaroslav Kalfar, and Vicki Gottlieb for their good eyes.

To Mr. Randall for making ninth-grade English so fun.

To my beantown boys Jason Brown, Kofi Thomas, Pashington Obeng, JP Jacquet, Nagib Charles, and Jose Vega.

To Prof. Robin DG Kelley and Alvin Blanco, for writing me great grad school recs.

To Farrah Griffin, for being such an elegant role model.

To Ebony Hayes, owner of Mind, Body, Hair, an urban oasis in the Bronx, for my locs.

To Brook Stephenson and Kimarlee Nguyen, rest peacefully.

About the Author

Sidik Fofana earned an MFA from New York University. Three of his stories have appeared in the *Sewanee Review*. He lives in New York City, where he is a public school teacher.